Would Alana destroy everything Lance and Stephanie had worked for?

Lance turned back to the dark-haired beauty behind him and said slowly, "Now let me get this straight. You want me to film the rest of the movie here?"

Alana nodded.

"And you want me to cancel my lease with Stephanie? And to place a lien against the property for the amount I have invested in it." He paused, almost choking on the words.

She nodded. "And Stephanie Haynes is to be replaced in the picture."

"I can't do that, Alana."

"Do what?"

"Submit to any of those demands."

"Very well. Then give up your option and lose your entire investment—which I happen to know amounts to all you have in this world, Lance." She shook her head. "You shouldn't have acted so foolhardily, dear. It isn't like you."

"Nor is this like you, Alana. Why? Why?"

"I told you. Love."

"Love doesn't destroy another person."

"If you mean Stephanie, it won't destroy her. She's young and beautiful, a survivor. But she's standing in the way of something the man I love wants, so she'll have to move over."

Doris English is no stranger to inspirational romance. Her first published romance was *The Challenged Heart*. *Free to Love* marks her debut as a *Heartsong Presents* author.

Free
to Love

Doris English

Heartsong Presents

ISBN 1-55748-462-7

FREE TO LOVE

PRINTED IN THE U.S.A.

one

Dread lay inside Stephanie Haynes like a weight of cold steel as she sat alone on her small balcony and stared into the mist that shrouded the boulder-strewn New England coast. Needles of morning light penetrated the grayness as the sun struggled to bring in the new day. This greeting of the morning was her daily ritual, but today anxiety clung to her like a rain-soaked blanket.

The aroma of fresh coffee wafted through the air, and she turned toward a soft rustling noise behind her. Stephanie's eyes met the steady gaze of Martha Newton, her aging housekeeper who stood in the open french doors separating the balcony from Stephanie's bedroom. She held a breakfast tray in her hands.

Martha set her heavy burden down on a green wrought-iron table beside Stephanie. "I heard you up, child, and knew you'd be needing this. With all the decisions you'll be making today, you'll need every ounce of strength you can muster."

"Decisions? Seems they have been made for me." Stephanie smiled wryly.

"The good Lord always gives us an option," Martha responded softly.

Silence held sway for a moment, as the steaming coffee added its vapor to the mist surrounding them and its pleasant odor to the pungent smells of sea and morning. Her voice husky, Stephanie responded, "I do have one, but I have a difficult time believing it's from Him."

"If you mean selling Boulder Bay to that Jay Dalton, then there must be another you haven't considered," Martha replied with a snort.

"There is, lose it to the bank." Stephanie turned toward the older woman and away from the roar of the invisible breakers, discouragement etched in the fatigue binding her young face.

"If you could just hold out a few more months, surely the inn would be on a paying basis," Martha encouraged.

One corner of Stephanie's mouth curved slightly upward in a sad, patient smile. "I can't. I don't have enough operating capital to see us through the month. The money I borrowed for renovations is due, and the bank has turned down an extension."

"Something about that situation sounds peculiar to me. This place should be ample collateral, and your plan to turn it into an inn is a good one. I thought banks were interested in sound investments." Martha's fine brows were drawn almost together in a disapproving frown.

"They seem to think my inexperience hinders the soundness of it."

"Pshaw! What's that got to do with it? You're a hard worker, I can vouch for that. I know the Lord don't want you to lose your home place to the bank. Why, it's been in the family for generations," Martha insisted.

Stephanie smiled sadly. "Ancestors don't count with a bank, profits do."

"Are you sure it's not someone who has his eye on this property trying to force you out?"

"I don't think so. It does take more than just hard work to make a business venture successful," Stephanie explained wistfully.

If only her father had followed through with his dream of turning Boulder Bay into a bed and breakfast! He, however, had refused to face the inevitable: The upkeep on the old inn was too expensive unless it could bring in a substantial income.

Martha, tall and slender as a willow reed, pursed her lips and sat down in a wrought-iron dining chair beside the table. The intricate acorn designs in the back of the chair held the morning moisture like slanted miniature finger bowls. Perched on the edge of the seat, her back ramrod straight, she poured the rich, mahogany beverage into a translucent china cup that had been Stephanie's great-grandmother's.

Martha cupped both her hands over the steaming cup to warm them. A long silence reigned before she remarked thoughtfully, "When you got that loan, Stephanie, I felt uneasy about the short time limit on it."

"That's all the bank would consider, but they did assure me that an extension would be no problem." Stephanie sounded perplexed.

"No one could finish what had to be done around here in six months. And on top of that, they wouldn't loan you nearly what you needed, while demanding the whole place as collateral," Martha insisted.

"The contractor didn't live up to his promised schedule, and then unexpected repairs cost more than anticipated. I guess I should have sold it." Stephanie shrugged her shoulders in defeat.

"Sold the old Haynes home place? Heaven forbid."

"What do you think I'm going to have to do today?" Stephanie asked, her brow creased, her wide blue eyes cloudy.

"Not sell it to Jay Dalton. Your parents, God rest their souls, would turn over in their graves if they knew a man like him was going to own Boulder Bay. Anyway, I heard he isn't buying it to live in," Martha rejoined as she reached over to replenish her cup.

"He told me he wanted it for a summer home. Don't you believe him?" Stephanie questioned, her eyes narrowed.

"No. I'd take anything that man said with a grain of salt until I had more proof than just his word. You just be careful about him."

Stephanie looked at the older woman, warm affection lighting her eyes. "If I sell, then I can salvage something from it, enough to live on until I can get a job. He's promised a place for you and John."

"What if we donated our services to you? We have a little nest egg we could loan you until you could get on your feet. . . "

"No," Stephanie interrupted.

"Why not?" Martha's quiet voice insisted.

"I won't take advantage of you, that's why not. The decision was mine, and I will not allow you to suffer for my mistakes."

"I won't listen to talk like that, Stephanie Haynes. No one knows better than a bank that it takes time and money to get a business started. Surely they'll give you an extension, but if not, then use our money. Anything to hold out a little bit longer. A little time, maybe more advertising, and I know we'd make it."

"But I haven't any more time. Even if we were ready to open right now, which we aren't, there's nothing to carry us until we're on a paying basis."

"I don't know why you're so stubborn about letting John and me help you." Pain was reflected in her eyes.

"Well, I can't let you take that risk. Boulder Bay has got to go. This is, after all, just a house. Sometimes life requires us to give up things that are important to us." Stephanie's brave words denied the bereavement she felt as a fresh onslaught of pain surged through her. She closed her eyes tightly, willing the truth away before her beloved friend could see it.

But Martha did see, and her gray eyes clouded as tears threatened. "Don't deny your feelings, my dear. This house and us are all that you have of your past. You've been too busy to let the grief of your parents' death catch up with you. Now it's all wrapped up together."

Stephanie's mouth felt dry and faintly tasted of salt from her tearful struggle throughout the night. Now her eyes stung as they held Martha's. "What am I ever going to do without your wisdom?"

Martha answered briskly, "You're not. We're family, and you aren't rid of us yet, little lady."

Stephanie smiled through a mist clouding her eyes. "Is that a fact?"

"Sure is. Tell you what, since you don't seem much in the mood for food, why don't you go down to the cove for a swim? Always did make you feel better. Now, mind you, be careful, it's a lonely place," Martha cautioned.

"Maybe it would help. I'll be careful. Anyway, since Dad died, no one but us even knows about the place. Maybe a swim will get the cobwebs out."

Martha smiled as she went out the door. "You need all the cobwebs out today, girl."

Stephanie was into her suit and out of the house in record

time. The sun had won its victory, and now her world shimmered in a soft golden radiance. She ran toward the bluff, which towered over the crashing breakers, and paused at the edge. A brisk breeze ruffled her long, silvery-blond hair, caressing her skin. To shield herself from the salty spray, she wrapped her arms around herself, hugging her form-fitting white swimsuit. Her eyes, now the color of the sky above, searched the horizon as if hoping to find in the clouds the answer to her dilemma.

She sighed and turned toward the house behind her. The brilliant morning light reflected off fresh paint and polished windows. From the widow's walk to the broad front porch with spindled railings and ornate fretwork, she took in every detail. She lingered, reluctant to tear herself away.

Finally she shook her head and took a deep breath, relishing the faint fragrance of an early blooming rose as it mingled with the briny sea. She turned to walk across the cold, smooth rock ledge toward a stone shelf that flared and swept out toward the sea, making a small crescent. Within the inner arc of the crescent, the path led downward through an opening like the eye of a needle, between huge boulders, then dropped steeply in natural cuts resembling shallow steps. The passageway ended at the edge of a secluded inlet of emerald green water.

Stephanie dropped the towel she held loosely in her hand and executed a perfect dive into the deep pool just below her. She surfaced, and turned over onto her back, letting the warm sun caress her face. Minutes slipped away before the knot in her stomach eased and peace usurped anxiety.

Here in her own private cove her father had taught her

to swim; here at Boulder Bay he had taught her about a God of love who watched over her and wanted to guide her. Stephanie knew then that God had calmed her fears.

She rolled over in the water and put her head down, channeling her newly found energy into slow, powerful strokes. The water barely rippled as she glided through the pool. She relished the gentle resistance, the challenge of her body against its silken embrace. At last ready to face the day, she reached out for the handholds, chiseled out years before.

Instead of touching smooth stone, strong hands grabbed hers and lifted her out of the water. Startled, Stephanie looked up into the bluest eyes she had ever encountered.

"I didn't know we had mermaids in the area." His voice, deep and resonant, bounced off the rock wall while his eyes danced with merriment.

Speechless, Stephanie strained to pull away from the stranger but he held her firmly in his grip. One small foot landed on the narrow step and then the other as he swung her into the steps below him. When she gained her balance, he loosened his hold.

"Where did you come from, and who are you?" she inquired, her voice weak with apprehension.

"Lancelot at your service. I rescue pretty maids, er, mermaids, that is," he replied with a crooked grin.

"I didn't need rescuing," she offered weakly. Alarm and curiosity battled in Stephanie's pounding heart. He released her hands.

"Perhaps not, but would you rob me of that pleasure and cheat both of us?"

Stephanie ignored his question, retorting sharply, "I don't know what you're doing here, but you are trespassing. This is private property, very private, in fact."

"Oh, not really, I have business here. I just didn't know it would be so pleasant."

"The only business you could have here would be at my invitation. I'm positive I didn't invite you."

Laughter lines crinkled at the corner of his eyes. "That's only because you didn't know me."

"Since I don't know you, would you be good enough to leave? You're blocking my exit, and I'm in a hurry." Her teeth began to chatter as rivulets of cold water ran down her body and formed puddles on the hard stone.

"You didn't seem in a hurry."

Stephanie held his eyes while her mind groped. She was alone in this hidden cove; no one could hear her if she cried out. Yet something about this stranger with electric blue eyes and sun-streaked hair intrigued more than frightened her.

"I watched you from there." He pointed to a shelf in the cliff. "You passed me and didn't even glance my way. Such deep thoughts!"

His eyes held hers. Her heart thudded strangely.

"I didn't expect an intruder."

"I'm intruding?"

She nodded, adding softly, "And now you're detaining me. Please let me pass."

The one-sided grin again parted his face as mischief burned in his eyes. "Come ahead."

Undaunted, the stranger stood with his feet firmly planted on the steps above her, leaving no room for escape.

Anger stirred in Stephanie, mysteriously mixing with fascination. Her flush deepened as she clinched her hand into a tight fist.

Obviously enjoying his advantage, the intruder crossed his arms and pursed his lips. Then tilting his head to the right, he calmly surveyed her from head to foot. He smiled slightly and nodded in a gesture of approval.

Fury blazed in Stephanie's narrowed eyes as she lifted her chin defiantly. She had two choices. She could continue standing here so close she felt the heat from his sun-warmed body or retreat to the pool below.

Not one to retreat, she reached up and grabbed for her towel now draped across the man's bare, bronzed shoulder. The violent movement proved too much for her narrow footing. Losing her balance, she fell backward, and the bright world of sun and sea gave way to silent blackness.

two

"Stephanie Haynes, what are you doing out of bed?" Martha's question seemed to echo off the walls of the airy Victorian bedroom. "You just turn right around and get yourself settled back in that bed of yours. Doc Andres said you're to take it easy for the next few days."

"Take it easy? What happened?" Stephanie rubbed her head gingerly, her hand encountering a mass of wet curls.

"You had a nasty fall. Don't you remember?"

"No, at least I don't remember falling, only. . . " Stephanie hesitated, unwilling to reveal more.

"Only what?"

"Oh, nothing. How did I fall?"

"When you went swimming. I shouldn't have suggested you go off by yourself. That always has worried me, but you were in such a state this morning and a swim always does you so much good." She paused with a long sigh, regret etched in her face. "If that Mr. Donovan hadn't been there to rescue you, then you'd not be worrying about anything else."

"Mr. Donovan rescued me? I don't know any Mr. Donovan." A puzzled frown wrinkled her brow as something in her subconscious tried to surface.

"Well, I don't either, but the good Lord surely sent him along at the right time. You know, the Good Book says the Lord looks after widows and orphans. All I know is I'm glad He sent that nice man your way just in time." Martha seemed to breathe a sigh of relief.

Suddenly with blinding clarity the brilliant blue eyes and laughing mouth of the morning took on substance. Weakly, Stephanie sat down on the bright-flowered chintz boudoir chair. "What did this rescuing angel look like?"

"Hmm, he was tall, real tall, berry brown skin with red-blond hair and blue eyes, the kind that send shock waves through a body." Martha felt her cheeks blush as if the handsome stranger were in the room.

"Some rescuing angel! He's the reason I fell. Didn't you wonder how he just *happened* to be there when I needed help?"

"Never thought much about it. Seems to me the Lord provides in strange and wondrous ways. I figured He knew you'd be needing help so He just sent it on ahead."

"Martha, I hate to dampen your faith, but the man caused me to fall," insisted Stephanie, her mind clamoring with the morning's events.

"Well, 'pears to me you're up here in this room and not at the bottom of the ocean," Martha retorted, unconvinced.

Stephanie stared at the older woman, nettled by her simple explanation. "If you could have seen your good looking angel a few minutes ago, you wouldn't be so certain who sent him."

The slender young woman took a deep breath and continued, her eyes pleading. "He nearly scared me to death. I didn't know he was anywhere around until I started to get out of the water. There he was, like some unwelcome, arrogant apparition, watching me swim. Furthermore, he blocked my path, refusing to leave. When I tried to pass him, my foot slipped, and that's the last thing I remember."

"All the same, he saved your life."

Exasperated, Stephanie responded shortly, "Didn't you hear anything I said? If he hadn't been there I wouldn't have fallen."

"Now we don't know that for sure, do we? All we do know is if he hadn't been there you wouldn't be here now."

Recognizing the impossibility of convincing Martha of anything once her mind was made up, Stephanie asked, "Who is this 'angel' and what was he doing here?"

"Child, I didn't have time to ask him all that. I was too busy getting my heart to settle down when I looked at you all limp and dead looking in his arms. Then I called the doctor and Mr. Donovan left, saying he'd see you, us, later. He called about thirty minutes later to see what the doctor said."

"He must not have been too concerned or he would have stayed," Stephanie pointed out wryly.

"No," said Martha hesitantly, her voice less convincing, "he was late for an appointment."

"Don't you think it was a little strange he didn't give you his full name?"

"I was so flustered, perhaps he did and I just can't recall."

"Probably not. He knew he had some responsibility in that accident."

"Well, just leave be. You're safe, and I'm more thankful than you could ever know. Me and John never had any children of our own and living here with you, watching you grow up, has made up for it. I can't tell any difference than if I'd really given birth to you. It's just like you are part ours." Martha reached out her hand to touch Stephanie's arm in an uncharacteristic show of affection.

A lump swelled in Stephanie's throat when she encountered the unvarnished love in Martha's eyes. "I know. I couldn't have made it without you. I realize the sacrifices you've made for me, especially after Dad's death and through Mother's illness."

"Sacrifices, humph!" Martha paused and cleared her throat. "I have been giving some more thought about your predicament while you've been laying here so still and helpless in this bed. What if John and I weren't around? You know we aren't getting any younger! It's time you started thinking about settling down somewhere and raising a family. Let some good man do the worrying for you. Today just proves my point." Martha punctuated the last with a brisk nod of her head.

Stephanie's smile faded and a guarded look replaced the brief sparkle in her blue eyes. "You're wrong on both counts, Martha. I don't need a man to do the 'worrying' for me. That's what happened to my mother. She couldn't cope when she lost Dad. She lived life from the passenger's side, but that's not for me. I want a career and independence, and that's what I intend to have. If I ever marry it will be on my own terms, not because I'm looking for someone to take care of me."

"Not even someone like Todd Andrews?"

"Todd?" Warm memories brightened Stephanie's eyes. "Todd was like a big brother to me, but I haven't seen him since I was fifteen and his family moved to Texas. Strange you should mention him, Martha. I received a letter from him yesterday."

"Not so strange. I saw the letter on your desk; made me think of him. Fine youngster as I recall."

"Todd was a dear. Did you know he graduated from law school at the top of his class? He's thinking about going into politics. Yet I wonder if I'd even recognize him. Sometimes the man doesn't fulfill the boyhood promise."

Stephanie stood up slowly and made her way gingerly to the bureau. Opening the top narrow drawer, she released a subtle fragrance of potpourri that Martha had made from crushed rose petals. Beneath the satin container she found a picture of Todd. He had been seventeen when the picture was taken. Tall and slender with broad shoulders, dark hair, a finely shaped nose, and a lopsided grin, he was a handsome teenager. The picture had failed to do justice to him, Stephanie mused silently. She couldn't see that special spark in his laughing eyes.

Martha gave her a quizzical look as she gazed intently at the photograph. "You can't make me believe he hasn't fulfilled all his promise, both in looks and character. His eyes fairly twinkled all the time, especially when he looked at you. Yes, mighty fine boy, that one."

"Martha!"

"Just observing, just observing. Don't get all riled up again. A body's got a right to some observations."

Stephanie's sternness dissolved in laughter. "Anyway, he's probably engaged by now although he didn't mention it in his letter. A while back he was pretty serious with the governor's daughter."

"That wouldn't surprise me any, he would be a real catch for any girl."

"Well, I'm not fishing, now or ever."

Ignoring Stephanie's retort, Martha remarked dryly, "Be that as it may, you'd better quiet down a little if you're going to make your appointment."

"I'd forgotten all about my appointment! Nothing like a brush with death to put things into perspective. What time is it? Oh, I've already missed it!" Stephanie glanced at her watch on the bureau beside her.

The older woman smiled warmly. "I called Mr. Jarrett and told him you couldn't make it this morning, and asked him to give you another appointment. He said fine, how about middle of the afternoon? I said only if you felt like it. He sounded kinda eager, if you know what I mean. Said if you couldn't make it down to the bank, perhaps he'd just drop by with the papers, but it's only 10:30 so you have plenty of time to rest. Maybe by this afternoon your headache should be easing off."

"Thank you for taking care of that," Stephanie replied softly, visibly touched by the older woman's care and concern.

"There's a lot more John and I could do for you to ease your burden if you'd let us. Your independence is going to cause you real heartache one of these days, I fear. Why don't you want anyone's help, honey?"

"Mom's love for Dad crippled her. Dad always handled everything, and Mom let him. He was her whole world, and when he died she didn't know how to survive." Involuntarily Stephanie shuddered, remembering her mother and the tragic year after her father's death.

"After she died, I had to make decisions for which they hadn't prepared me. If I'd had any idea about how critical our financial situation was, I'd never have stayed at college the last year. I could have invested that money in Boulder Bay. I guess there's no use in rehashing the 'what might have beens'."

"I told you we would forego our pay until you could afford it," Martha reminded.

"You've already helped out more than you should

have." Stephanie closed her eyes, fighting to control her emotions. "I won't, I can't, take advantage of anyone, most of all someone I love. " She paused, adding firmly, "This is my problem, not yours. You will not suffer because of my mistakes."

The older woman looked sadly into Stephanie's eyes for a long moment, then walked over to her and patted her hand. Stephanie dropped her head, refusing to look into Martha's eyes. Why was she afraid to accept people's help? Was she, as Martha indicated, afraid to love and be loved?

She shuddered slightly and pulled her light robe closer as the thought sent a chill through her in the room warmed by a late spring sun.

Martha looked pensively at Stephanie, sympathy and affection mingling in her blue-gray eyes. As she walked toward the door, she gave one last gentle command. "You get back in bed. I'll awaken you in plenty of time for lunch and your meeting."

Hours later at Martha's light tap Stephanie was aroused from a deep sleep. Struggling to dispel the grogginess that plagued her, she opened her eyes wide and stretched her arms high above her head, noting with pleasure that her headache was only a memory.

A pot of steaming tea greeted Stephanie as Martha revealed a lunch tray filled with chicken salad and fresh fruit. Her stomach growled a hearty welcome to the tantalizing aroma of fresh baked bread and apple muffins.

When she had finished she lingered at the window, putting off her shower, reluctant to get ready for her dreaded appointment. She could see no way out. The quarterly mortgage payment came due on Monday, and not only did she not have the money to pay it, she did not have enough operating capital to carry her through the next month. Once the sale was completed and the mortgage paid off, she would see what was left to finish her education.

She sighed and stood up slowly, pausing to glance in her bureau mirror. *"What will I do when I sell Boulder Bay?"* Shaking her head at her reflection, she wrinkled her nose. *"Mr. Jarrett has been too evasive about how much Mr. Dalton is willing to pay,"* she thought.

After a leisurely shower, Stephanie applied her make-up sparingly. Her even tan emphasized her blue eyes so she only needed a light shadow on her eyelids and a brief touch of mascara. The weight she had lost made her high cheek bones more prominent.

In college she had been dubbed "the beauty," but she never gave it much thought. She was accustomed to the approving appraisal of men but she chose to ignore such gestures, dismissing them as a fact of life rather than a tribute to her true beauty.

That is until today. The encounter at the cove disturbed her in more ways than one. True, the invasion of her special sanctuary had annoyed her. But if she admitted the truth, it was the man himself, the way he looked at her and the way she felt when her eyes met his that was the real problem. Even now the memory brought a blush to her face. She grinned sheepishly. "Martha was right. Those cobalt eyes do send shock waves through you."

His eyes as they met hers were daring, challenging, yet admiring all at the same time. Was that what triggered the angry response so uncharacteristic of her? Or perhaps it was fear, but fear of what? Her safety? The light bronze of Stephanie's face deepened. Or was it her heart? Was she afraid of the woman's heart that thundered a response her actions denied? Did the encounter stir up embers she had buried long ago under heartache and furious activity?

Stephanie paused to consider her reflection before carefully placing the mascara wand into its small cylinder. She tilted her head to one side and leaned closer to the mirror. "Stephanie, my dear, you acted like an outraged spinster," she said out loud with a brittle laugh.

The sound of her voice startled her in the silent room. Yet not even this moment of truth could wipe out the memory of her first encounter with those deep blue eyes. She continued her conversation with the young woman in the mirror. "I'm not some love-starved female who thinks the primary purpose of life is to find a man. So what if he was extraordinary looking, I've never behaved like that before!" She shook her head, denying that the vitality emanating from the man, even his very nearness, had disturbed her.

An overwhelming curiosity forced her to search her image for what had caused him to look at her as he did. After gazing at her reflection for several seconds, she shrugged as she grabbed her shining mass of golden curls and captured them in a tight chignon. *I don't know what he saw because I don't know what he was looking for*, she thought suddenly.

As she surveyed her reflection one last time, a wry smile of acknowledgment looked back. From this day forward life would never be the same. She turned and reached for a jacket to cover her pale blue linen dress. She squared her shoulders, ready to meet her destiny, oblivious that she was a remarkably beautiful and elegant woman.

three

The heavy oak side door leading to the outside groaned as
Stephanie pushed it open. She made a mental note to oil
the hinges, then winced as she remembered what today
would bring. Her dream had ended, or at least it would
when she arrived in town and finished her business. After
today any repairs or problems would be up to Mr. Jay
Dalton.

She looked longingly toward the path that hugged the
bluff and made its way into town following the curve of the
shore below. A slight smile tugged at one corner of her
mouth, dimpling her cheek as she yielded to the temptation to walk to town instead of drive. Impulsively she
found herself overlooking the sea on her way to town.

The bluff was high above the water, and the low tide left
a wide strip of sand and rocks far below her. The salty
breeze that blew in felt cool against her skin and an
occasional gust set her skirts whirling around her legs.

Anyone who enjoyed the rugged beauty of a long,
oceanfront property with relative seclusion, yet still
conveniently close to town belonged at Boulder Bay. How
could she blame Jay Dalton for wanting it? Stephanie
sighed. Maybe he would buy it, but the walk to town
reinforced her resolve to get all that she could from her
place. If she had to lose it, she would fight for what it was
worth.

Stephanie arrived at the offices of Brown, Jarrett, and

Garrard in good spirits and calm of heart and mind. She had come to terms with herself and accepted the inevitable. Every eye in the plush offices turned toward her as she entered. Some appraised furtively, and some openly, but none ignored her beauty and sun-kissed radiance.

Stephanie approached the desk nearest the door where the only woman in the room sat. A sign on her desk designated her as executive assistant, and the expensive perfume she wore teased the air around her desk, giving Stephanie a moment of envy.

For an instant she wished for the trappings of success, a designer suit and accessories to match, an expensive perfume, something to lift her from the rural, homespun image she felt she presented.

The young woman looked up and smiled with a disarming friendliness, dispelling her cool mystique. "May I help you?"

Stephanie hesitated, glancing around the room, as she looked for Mr. Jarrett among the men seated at the adjacent desks. Her eyes went to each desk and every man, in turn, lowered his head, reluctantly taking his eyes from her.

"Mr. Jarrett? I had an appointment?" she asked, a perplexed look darkening her eyes.

"Oh, you must be Miss Haynes. Mr. Jarrett's expecting you. I'm Abigail Burnes, his assistant. Mr. Dalton is not here yet. Would you like to go on in anyway?"

"Yes, I would, thank you," Stephanie responded.

Abigail pushed her chair away from her desk of finely crafted cherry and stood up. "I'll show you to his office. I need a break. Would you like a cup of coffee?"

"No, thank you. This is the first time I've been to your

new offices. Are you enjoying them?"

"Well, yes and no," replied the pretty brunette, her voice lowered intentionally. Her smile invited camaraderie, dispelling the last remnants of Stephanie's uneasiness.

"How's that?"

The young assistant looked over her shoulder and then said in a voice just above a whisper, "In our old office the decor was fluorescent lights and utility working space, you know, metal desk and blinds, but I had my own private cubicle. In here the esthetics are wonderful, but the open work area can be distracting, not to mention my hair has to be in place and my make-up perfect all the time. I feel like one of the company's displays."

Stephanie laughed at the amused indignation mirrored on her face and commented, "I can see your point, but then they have a very impressive display with you. You fit right into these plush surroundings, but I guess it would be difficult working in a room full of men and having so little privacy."

"Yes, it's my privacy that I miss. Working for Mr. Jarrett is a dream though, I couldn't have a better boss. Are you a secretary?"

"Not at the moment, but I will be needing a job shortly. Do you have an opening?"

The young woman looked at Stephanie and smiled warmly. "Not right now, but I've heard rumors of expansion. If my workload increases I'll need an assistant. Why don't you check back with me?"

"You say you've heard rumors of expansion?"

"Oh, yes, we are going to handle all the real estate for the area from North Shore to Emerald Shore, about a 500-square-mile area. With all the new plans underway, we're expecting a virtual boom."

"What new plans?"

"Didn't you know this area just legalized gambling?"

"I would hardly call that an asset."

"Well, that's a surprise, I mean, since your business is with Mr. Dalton." Abby nervously twisted her single strand of creamy white pearls.

"What do you mean?" Stephanie asked, her eyes narrowing slightly as Martha's warning echoed in the corridors of her mind.

"Didn't you know he is the biggest casino owner on the East Coast?" Abby's voice was insistent, tinged with a slight impatience.

Stephanie stopped midstep. "No, as a matter of fact, I didn't. I only talked to him once when he came to look my place over."

"Some of the guys in our firm said if he moves in here, the sky's the limit on development property. This coastline is beautiful and undeveloped. With a casino as a drawing card we could have a thriving tourist trade all year long. Consider what that would do for land values."

"Pardon me, Abigail, but where would you put a casino in Emerald Cove?"

"Well, you know, your. . . ." The color drained from Abigail's face as she looked directly into Stephanie's puzzled eyes, understanding replacing impatience. "You really didn't know?"

"Know what?"

Abigail stopped just as they arrived outside Howard Jarrett's door. "Sometimes I talk too much. Miss Haynes, do me a favor. Don't let Mr. Jarrett know I said anything to you. It could cost me my job."

Stephanie took a deep breath as she reached for the door. "Of course not. You've done me a real service, but you're wrong on one count. Gambling, legalized or not, can never be a boon to a community. It brings crime and greed and they're no assets ever, land values notwithstanding."

Abigail paused before turning away and looked steadily at Stephanie. "I never thought of it like that. Maybe we could talk again sometime."

"I'd love to. How long have you lived in Emerald Cove?" Stephanie probed.

"Only six months. I came here from the home office and so far I don't know anyone my own age." Abigail sighed.

"Well, we'll remedy that, Abigail. Call me, and we'll get together," Stephanie said over her shoulder as she turned to open the door that led into the large, cherry-paneled office of Howard Jarrett.

His back was to her as he talked on the phone and stared out a window behind his desk. From the floor-to-ceiling window Stephanie could see a lush green lawn sloping gently to meet a rocky bluff that then fell sharply to the sea. Stephanie's heart constricted at the thought of this gentle hamlet being transformed into a "Las Vegas-by-the-sea." That would explain why this large and prosperous firm had chosen this little village to build its fine imposing offices.

Howard Jarrett, a handsome man in his midfifties, whirled around when he heard the door close and rose from his desk as he placed the telephone in its cradle.

Stephanie watched the distinguished looking man with salt-and-pepper hair walk briskly around his imposing mahogany desk, his hands outstretched. They were as smooth and well manicured as a woman's. A gold watch embossed with diamonds encircled his wrist while a plain gold wedding band gleamed softly on his ring finger. He smelled faintly of pipe tobacco.

"Stephanie, my dear, are you all right?" he asked, concern showing in his hazel eyes.

"I'm fine, Mr. Jarrett," Stephanie said assuredly as she offered her hand to him.

"Please call me Howard. Dalton will be here shortly but I wanted to talk to you about his offer before he arrives. It really is quite generous, and since you seem anxious to sell, my advice is to accept it. I can assure you that it exceeds the average price of land in the area by several hundred dollars an acre."

"How much is he offering, Mr. Jarrett?"

Howard Jarrett paused, then with a confident smile pointed to the tufted leather wing back chair. "Have a seat, my dear. That one's comfortable. Would you like a cup of coffee?"

"The offer, Mr. Jarrett?" Stephanie insisted as she sat down.

"Oh, yes. Your house is quite large, twenty-five rooms, I believe. However, its age and the renovations and upkeep have to be considered. Even though you have twenty acres of oceanfront property, much of it is quite rugged, you know."

"Mr. Jarrett!"

"Howard, my dear."

"Howard, I'm familiar with my property. What I'm not acquainted with is Mr. Dalton's offer. I can't understand why you wanted to have this meeting before you had even given me an offer to consider. If I'm not interested then you've wasted all our time," Stephanie responded firmly.

"You'll be interested," he said confidently.

"How much?"

"How about a million dollars?" he responded, his eyes burning with triumphant expectation.

Stephanie wrinkled her brow and narrowed her eyes. The silence grew heavy as she purposely delayed her response.

Howard Jarrett's confident stance weakened slightly. As the seconds passed without comment from Stephanie, he began to squirm and finally blurted out, "Well, what about it?"

The young woman widened her eyes and said softly with a cool smile, "I'm interested." The sum was three times what she needed to clear and over twice as much as she had even dared hope for. Yet, a warning signal sounded deep within her and she added firmly, "Now tell me this. Why is he willing to pay that much for an old house on twenty acres of rugged property?"

Howard Jarrett's handsome, tanned face flushed slightly and his well-manicured fingers drummed a nervous rhythm on his desk. He had not expected her response. "Well, Stephanie, it's just a matter of his seeing it and falling in love with the quaint old place. It's secluded, and he needs a quiet place away from his many business ventures. You know what I mean, a place to get away."

"But what precisely does he want to do with Boulder Bay?"

"I just told you."

"No, you told me why he likes it, but you didn't actually say what he was going to do with it."

Howard Jarrett's suave facade cracked as he answered thinly, "He will repair it and use it for a summer home. Now let me tell you, Miss Haynes, you will never get a better offer, and if you don't accept this, you'll have to find another agent."

Stephanie's composure remained unruffled. "You're telling me that if I don't accept this offer, you will no longer work for me and our agreement is broken?"

The agent nervously put both hands to his temples and ran them back through his hair. "Yes, that is exactly right. I'm a very busy man, and I have many other clients who know what they want and follow my advice."

Stephanie nodded her head and said pleasantly, "Fine. I just wanted to make certain I understood what you meant."

"Well?" Jarrett asked with one eyebrow slightly arched.

"Well, what?"

"Are you ready to sign this contract?" he asked, irritation elevating his voice.

"Not until Mr. Dalton arrives," she replied.

"I see," he snapped. "Just understand this. Mr. Dalton won't put up with delaying tactics so you better make up your mind before he walks in that door. If you keep Jay Dalton waiting for an answer, he'll just go buy someplace else."

"There is no place like mine, Mr. Jarrett," Stephanie quietly reminded him. "Except for the town and my property, the government owns all the adjacent shoreline. No, he'll have to go to another state."

Howard Jarrett narrowed his eyes. "Who's been talking to you, Stephanie?"

"What do you mean, Howard? Did you think I was totally uninformed about the value and desirability of my property?" If the truth were told, Stephanie was amazed that these words had come from her mouth. Sometime during her walk to town she had decided to fight for what the place was worth. Her inner alarm, which had sounded earlier, propelled her through this confrontation.

With a knock on the door, Abigail ushered in Jay Dalton. Stephanie had only seen him once and the encounter had been too brief to form an opinion. Now she studied him carefully, bearing in mind Martha's warning. He was a handsome man in a flamboyant sort of way. The cut of his clothes reflected a designer's touch, but he lacked the natural grace to wear them with ease. His dark, longish hair complemented his rugged features and swarthy complexion. Only his eyes captured Stephanie's attention. They were the lightless color of aged steel.

He breezed in the room with an outstretched hand and blustery greeting to Jarrett. However, when he turned his attention to Stephanie, he paused midsentence and looked at her from head to toe. With a smile of approval, he murmured, "How could I have forgotten such beauty? Howard, this is one deal I should have handled myself."

Stephanie smiled coolly, never taking her eyes from his. "Mr. Jarrett tells me I must not delay. Shall we get on with it, Mr. Dalton?"

"Howard is sorely mistaken. I'll always have time for you, Miss Haynes. Shall we say dinner this evening?"

"Oh, I think we can surely finish before then, Mr. Dalton."

"That would disappoint me. Perhaps we should view the property again?"

"Are you reconsidering your offer?"

"No, no, just a joke. Where are the papers? We sign, yes? Then we go to celebrate our good fortune. I get what I want, and you get a good price for it, eh?"

"I have one question, Mr. Dalton. What are you going to use Boulder Bay for?"

"Like I told your housekeeper, as a summer home."

"There are rumors that you want to turn it into a casino."

"Rumors, rumors, why would I want another? I have more than I can look after now. No, just a home."

"I see. Well then, I guess we have a deal. The price is very generous. Where are the papers, Mr. Jarrett?"

"Howard," corrected the agent regaining his composure.

"Howard, I'm ready to sell. It's a hard thing for me to sell my home. My family has owned it for generations."

"Yes, yes, I'm sure it must be. Now if you will sign right here, Stephanie, and Jay has his check, then we can finish this business satisfactorily for all of us." Relief washed across his face.

"One more thing, Mr. Dalton." Stephanie paused pen in hand. "If you are going to use my place for a summer home, then you'll have no objection to signing an affidavit that you do not intend to use it for a casino. Is that right?"

The rhythmic tick of the ornate walnut wall clock pierced the silence like a dagger. Alarm seized Jarrett's face as Jay Dalton responded smoothly, "My dear, I can't possibly see what that has to do with our deal. I refuse to sign an affidavit, because if my word isn't sufficient then the deal's off."

Stephanie cocked her head, smiled sweetly, and stood up. "Thank you for your time, gentlemen. We don't have a deal."

Jay Dalton turned his intense gaze on Stephanie, his former good humor replaced by an icy stare. "Miss Haynes, if this is a ploy for more money, it won't work."

"Believe me, it isn't. Your offer is fair, and I have no complaints. I only require an affidavit."

He paused for a long moment, then as Stephanie took a step toward the door, he spoke. "How does two million dollars sound to you along with relocating you anywhere you wish to live?" A low gasp escaped the realtor and he slumped in his seat.

"An affidavit *and* one million dollars is the deal, Mr. Dalton."

Jarrett looked in helpless frustration from one to the other, then jumped to his feet and exclaimed in disbelief, "Stephanie, what are you doing? I have the information on your loan before me. You are going to lose your place to the bank if you don't sell it. Be reasonable!"

"I know it doesn't seem sane to either of you, but there can be no other terms. I must have an affidavit, or I won't sell."

"I don't understand, Miss Haynes. Why can't you sell on my terms? I've doubled the price, and you've got to sell."

"Because I couldn't live with myself if I gained at the expense of a community I love."

"Who set you up as judge and jury to decide what's best for this town?" Jarrett asked.

"No one, Mr. Jarrett, but I do have a responsibility to others for my decisions."

He looked at her, his hazel eyes now cold with malice and anger. "Are you your brother's keeper?"

"Sometimes" was her sad response.

Dalton interrupted with a sneer. "You can't stop me."

"Perhaps not, but I refuse to aid you."

Then he laughed coldly. "Well, Miss Haynes, I tried to

do you a favor. Now I'll just wait for the bank to repossess it and sell it on the courthouse steps. I'll buy it then and save myself a bundle. You'll get nothing."

Stephanie walked toward the door. "No, you won't, Mr. Dalton. Somehow I'll keep it." She closed the door without a backward glance toward the two stunned men, and walked quickly down the hall past Abigail Burnes' vacant desk. Desire to leave this coastal compound of plush offices consumed her, but her trembling legs refused to cooperate. Seeking a place of escape, she turned toward town and the Hotel Atlantic Tea Room. There she could get a strong cup of tea and a place to sit until somehow her strength renewed.

Now what am I going to do, Lord? That was my only way out. Dalton's right, he can buy my place cheaper if it's repossessed. Yet, how can I sell it knowing what it will be used for? her mind questioned.

Stephanie stepped into the welcoming coolness of the tearoom and walked toward a table next to the window. A few white sails visible on the horizon prompted a fleeting urge to rig up *Carefree,* her sloop, and go for a sail.

Stephanie shook her head. No, she couldn't escape. She was trapped with no apparent way out. What was she to do? *Lord, You promised to meet all our needs, and I really have a need right now,* her heart pled silently.

Stephanie ordered tea and scones from Janie, the hostess, and, as an afterthought, requested the afternoon paper. The tea and scones revived her and with a deep sigh she turned to the want ads. Job opportunities appeared few and far between.

"I didn't know mermaids drank tea," said a voice behind her that set her heart to racing.

Stephanie turned and looked up into the mocking eyes of the man at the cove. Before she could respond, he lifted one long leg over the low-backed chair and sat down at her table.

"You!" she said through clenched teeth.

"Yep, it's me!" Undaunted by her narrowed eyes and bristling anger, he gave her a maddening grin.

"Why don't you have a seat, Mr. Mystery," she responded sarcastically.

"Donovan, Lance Donovan is my name and, thank you, I don't mind if I do. How are their scones?" he asked, taking the last one and smearing it liberally with strawberry jam. "Nearly good as my mother's, but of course nobody could hold a candle to hers."

"Won't you have the rest of my tea also?" she invited, her outrage at the man's arrogant boldness growing by the second.

"No, thanks, that won't hurt you. I'm eating this scone because you've had enough calories. Don't want you to gain any weight, you're just right!"

Stephanie's mouth flew open, shock at his impudence widening her eyes. For a moment the memory of a sneering Jay Dalton evaporated as she felt her early morning rage stir once again.

Donovan leaned across the table, placed his finger under her chin, and pushed upward, closing her mouth. "Don't gape. We need to talk. I've got a proposition for you."

Stephanie closed her eyes, her long dark lashes resting on her cheeks, and shook her head as if to clear her mind of this disturbing apparition. When she opened her eyes he still sat there, munching on the last remnant of her scone and smiling jauntily.

"A proposition?" Then Stephanie slowly nodded her head. "That figures."

"Good, now we can get down to business."

"Mr. Donovan," she responded weakly, "you'd be the last man I'd be interested in."

Lance looked at her, his brow slightly wrinkled. "Oh!" he exclaimed, laughing, understanding brightening his countenance. "Not that kind of proposition. I mean a business proposition."

"Business, what kind of business? You don't look like a business-man to me," she retorted, then added, "or act like one."

"Why? Is Jay Dalton your idea of a businessman?" he queried, his head cocked to one side.

Stephanie sighed with disgust. "Okay, okay. Tell Mr. Dalton I am not interested, and your, er, charm won't convince me either."

"Well, that's a relief. I'd heard rumors, and then when I saw Dalton go in Brown, Jarrett and Garrard right after you did, I thought I was too late."

"Have you been following me?"

"Well, yes and no, but not intentionally. You see, I had some business in town, and when I saw you go in their offices, I just decided to wait around."

"I still don't understand. Don't you work for Dalton?"

"Not on your life. I make an honest living. I'm Lancelot Donovan, movie producer."

"Yes, and I'm Joan of Arc."

"No, seriously, here's my card."

Stephanie took the card and read, *Century Production, Lancelot Donovan, President, Hollywood, California.* An amused smile momentarily softened her eyes as she looked up. With one side of her mouth twisted upward, she gave a derisive half chuckle. "Lancelot? You mean your name is really Lancelot?"

Donovan's jaunty confidence weakened, and he gave a crooked smile. "Yeah, my mom liked to read medieval novels." He shrugged before continuing quickly. "I'm Lance to my friends, but being in the movie business I felt that Lancelot had a certain show biz ring to it."

"Around here a name like Lancelot wouldn't be to your advantage. Anyway, anyone can print business cards."

"True, but these are genuine. I am who it says."

"You're a long way from home" was her skeptical retort.

"I am producing a new film and have been searching the northeastern coast for the right location. When I discovered Boulder Bay, I went to the courthouse and found out that it belonged to one Stephanie Haynes, but local gossip said she had sold it to Jay Dalton."

"What if I don't believe you, Mr. Donovan? You know a name like Lancelot makes it a little more difficult." Stephanie pressed her advantage, suddenly enjoying piercing the arrogance of this handsome stranger.

"Well, call Hollywood and check me out, but meanwhile read your local paper. Don't you keep up with the news?" he asked pointedly, attempting to divert the conversation.

"I've been preoccupied lately."

"Look on page one, or do you only read want ads?" Sarcasm dripped from his words like jam from a warm scone.

Stephanie pressed her lips together tightly and glared at

him as she turned the paper. True to his prediction, a small blurb announced in bold letters, FILM COMPANY SEARCHES.

"That's old news now, I've found what I want. It's Boulder Bay and you!" he exclaimed with boyish exuberance, extinguishing all traces of his former attitude.

"Really?" Stephanie asked, curiosity softening her retort.

"Yes, really. If you read the article you'll see I was searching for a location and a new face for the ingenue role. I've spent these past weeks walking shorelines, sailing in and out of coves, and auditioning women. I saw your place from a copter last week, and after I rented a sail boat and looked at it from the sea, I was fairly sure I'd found it. Today when I 'trespassed' and walked over it, I knew my search was over. How much do you want for it?" Pausing, he looked at her with mischief dancing in his eyes and added, "By the way, that cove is perfect for a love scene, don't you think?"

"I'm not believing this conversation!" Stephanie replied, trying not to laugh.

"So? Just name a price. I'll make a believer out of you!"

"It's not for sale to you at any price!" she responded as visions of gambling tables in her parlor came crashing back.

"Why? You'd rather do business with Mr. Dalton?"

"No, but what would be the difference between you and him?"

"I don't want it for the same reason he does."

"How do you know what he wants it for?" Stephanie queried, her brows furrowed.

"I told you, Ms. Haynes, I did a thorough investigation," Donovan assured. "It is for sale, isn't it?"

"I'm—I'm not sure," she stammered.

"Oh, it's me." He laughed as his steady gaze locked on hers. "Lovely lady, you'd better get used to me. I see a great future for us."

Stephanie stared at him in wide-eyed disbelief, then dropped her eyes before he could see her obvious embarrassment. She had read something in his eyes that stirred a strange, disturbing emotion within her. "This is all so sudden, Mr. Donovan. I need time to think."

"How about my coming by later this evening? Give you time to check out my credentials," he suggested pleasantly, all his former arrogant jauntiness missing.

Stephanie slowly nodded. "I guess that would be all right."

"About eight-thirty, then?" he pressed and acknowledged her fleeting nod. "Would you like a lift home?"

"No, thank you. I need the walk and time to think," she replied.

He reached across the table and picked up the check. Standing up, he almost whispered, "See you tonight."

four

The shadows lengthened and the breezes cooled as dusk arrived. Stephanie paced restlessly in the large parlor of Boulder Bay, her heart stirred by a faint hope that her head battled to deny.

On one side of the parlor nestled into the alcove formed by the three bay windows was a large storage chest of fine, old walnut. She sat down on it and listened to the distant roar of the tumultuous sea as it broke against the rocks. The intensity of the waves matched her mood. The answers she sought still eluded her; the steadfast faith that usually calmed her was missing.

Lance Donovan's credentials had checked out, and she had no problem with his intended use of the place. Furthermore, his films were notably wholesome and family oriented. So, what was her problem?

The doorbell interrupted her thoughts, and she stood up. She saw Donovan's profile outlined behind the lace-curtained glass of the old front door. Reluctantly, Stephanie walked across the heart pine floors of orange and gold as the lingering fragrance of lemon oil polish of antique furniture gave an inaudible welcome.

Tonight, however, her eyes saw nothing but the waiting profile, while her heart knew nothing but the anguish of indecision.

Lance stared quietly for a moment into Stephanie's eyes. A softer, warmer expression replaced his usual arrogance and somehow it comforted and reassured her. As if he sensed her indecision he suggested, "Let's go for a walk. I find sitting by the sea sometimes clears my mind."

She nodded, and they walked together silently, each deep in thought. They approached a bench placed strategically at the highest point of the property with a commanding view of the coast. Sitting a few inches apart, they lingered in a companionable silence until Lance turned to her, carefully choosing his words. "Stephanie, I've thought a great deal about our conversation this afternoon. I am withdrawing my offer to buy Boulder Bay."

Stephanie turned her face toward him and bit her bottom lip, waiting for his explanation. She knew then that caution had lost its battle with hope. Lance Donovan's profile had become a beacon in the gathering twilight, but with these words despair threatened to engulf her.

He smiled when he saw her expression, some of his jauntiness returning. "I have a better plan. What would you like to do if you didn't sell your place?"

"If you've done your homework, you know I have to sell it."

"You didn't answer my question," he gently insisted.

Stephanie turned away from him before he could see tears of longing mist her eyes. "I'd live here and have the most unique inn on the North Shore."

He put his hand under her chin and turned her face around to meet his, lifting it so he could look deeply into her eyes. "Then do it."

"I can't."

"Suppose you had a partner?"

"I don't know anyone who would be interested."

"But I do," he smiled.

"You? I thought you wanted to buy it for location."

"I did, but leasing it would be better for me and, I believe, for you in the long run. I thought it would be nice for a personal retreat, but the property is really too valuable to leave idle. Leasing it wouldn't give you enough money for your immediate needs, but what if I bought in as a partner and supplied the funds for renovations? Then I'd have an investment in an income-producing property. We'd both get what we want. I could have it when I wanted it, and you could have it after we leave. The movie company could stay on location and rent the facilities. Do you think your staff could handle accommodations for thirty-five or forty people?" Eagerness raised the timbre of his voice a pitch and washed his face in boyish anticipation.

"We don't have enough room in the main house to lodge them, but if the cottages were renovated we would. But Mr. Donovan, are you sure? What kind of money are you talking about?" She would leave no stone unturned.

"As much as you need," he gently assured.

"Sounds too good to be true," Stephanie responded, doubt darkening her eyes.

"There is one condition. I want to give you a screen test for the supporting actress role in my film. When I saw you this morning, I knew you were the lady of my dreams."

"Me, a movie star? I'm not the type," she objected, shaking her head.

"Depends on what you mean," he said.

"Glamorous, beautiful, sophisticated." Stephanie sighed.

"If you mean a glittering facade, no, you're not. What you have is the very essence of beauty: all the physical attributes put together with an intangible inner radiance that I had given up on finding," he explained, his tone one of sincere persuasion.

Stephanie tilted her head and stared at him. "Are you putting me on?"

"No, why did you think I looked at you the way I did this morning?"

"I don't know, but I felt like a side of meat that had just passed inspection," she retorted, pulling her mouth in a thin line as she relived her morning encounter.

"You had passed my wildest expectations. The world of films is a marketplace for beauty."

"Mr. Donovan, I'm not for sale," Stephanie responded primly.

"Miss Haynes, you've made that abundantly clear more than once today," he agreed with a chuckle. "Now what about my proposition, are you interested?"

"Could you call it something else? That particular term just doesn't appeal to me." She gave him a timorous smile, and for the first time the glow of expectation widened her eyes.

"How about 'business venture?'"

"That's better," she laughed, turning to look up at him with her eyes shining.

"Careful, don't look at me like that; you'll take my breath away," he said, smiling. "Well? I'm still waiting for my answer."

"The first part about leasing the inn for a filming location and housing the crew sounds wonderful, almost too good to be true. But I'm having problems with the other part about your financing it and my being in the movie."

"Why?"

"Lance, I won't take advantage of anyone and that plan sounds like you would be carrying 80 percent of the load. It's either charity or. . .what's in it for you? You see, I would be dependent on you."

He gave her a mock leer but said nothing.

"No, I'm serious. I refuse to be dependent on anyone. I've got to carry my load." Suddenly anxiety and weariness dimmed her eyes.

"Okay, I'm serious, too. In the first place I'm not a very charitable person even for beautiful damsels in distress. I'm a businessman. Here I see an opportunity for a profitable business venture, and you must have thought so too or you wouldn't have attempted it." Lance's eyes held hers, willing Stephanie to see she had nothing to fear.

"Well, yes, but I didn't have the capital."

"I do," Lance assured.

The final light of day had exited and a tall security light behind their bench bathed the couple in gold. For a moment silence reigned as Stephanie considered what Lance had said. The ocean's roar and a whippoorwill's loud rhythmic call from the woods interrupted her brief reverie. The brisk sea breeze ruffled her hair and lightly kissed her lips with salt as she breathed in the familiar smell of seaweed. She shivered and Lance moved cautiously toward her.

Taking off his jacket, he moved his arm across the bench behind her and draped his jacket over her shoulders. Then with a disarming smile he kept his arm around her. Stephanie turned toward him, seemingly unaware of his jacket, his arm behind her, and even oblivious to his nearness. Circumstances had invaded her comfort zone, threatening extinction of life as she knew it. Now Lance offered a promise of rescue that seemed too good to be true. Carefully she weighed the issues, groping for an answer as she searched for the right questions.

"What if there isn't a return on your money?" Stephanie probed.

"That won't happen, Stephanie. I'll be around often enough to go over the books and make suggestions. About the part in the movie, you would do well to read the magazines. Several articles have described in detail what I was looking for. . . ." He paused and took her face in his hands once again. "Go look in the mirror, Stephanie, and don't fail to thank God for what He's done for you."

"What if I can't act?" she insisted, willing him to persuade her.

His somber look gave way to a confident smile. "Then I'll teach you."

Stephanie turned from him and looked toward the navy horizon where stars twinkled like millions of diamonds. She sat transfixed for several moments, drinking in the familiarity, the beauty. Now she fought the urge to give in, to end the probing, but she knew she couldn't. Her decision had to be right.

Stephanie pulled her eyes from the stars and, dropping her head, asked hesitantly, almost inaudibly, "But what if you really want to do something else with Boulder Bay, something that I wouldn't approve of? How could I stop you?"

Lance shifted on the bench beside her and stretched his long legs out in front of him as he put his hands behind his neck. "You have a valid point. You don't know me, and I could have other plans for the place. What if I just lease it from you for the duration of the film and loan you the money for renovation and advertising? Then I will have the mortgage on it instead of the bank, and you can pay me back with interest or with part ownership of the inn, whichever suits you better. That way you retain control."

"Like I just asked, what's in it for you? That looks like a rather lopsided deal to me."

"Don't forget, you have to promise to be in my film if the screen test is okay. But beyond that, I see an opportunity for a business investment. You see, I'm confident when you observe firsthand my business acumen, and, of course, fall victim to my many charms, you will beg me to come into the business with you. We could have a real winner up on this bluff with the gorgeous view. Well, what do you think?"

Without warning relief coursed through Stephanie, washing away all vestiges of doubt. A sense of direction and confidence replaced the turmoil that had buffeted her off and on since she turned down Jay Dalton's offer. She sighed as if a heavy weight had lifted from her, and her shoulders relaxed against Lance's arm.

He felt the tension ease from her as she turned to look him squarely in the face. "I think I'm very interested." Then a mischievous grin suddenly lighted her face as she added, "I think you are an answer to prayer."

Lance flinched and raised his eyebrows. "Baby, you are full of surprises. I've been called a lot of things in my brief life, but an answer to prayer has never been one of them."

Laughing gently she remembered her earlier conversation with Martha and observed, "Lance, sometimes the Lord chooses strange avenues to perform His works."

With mock disappointment he responded, "Oh shucks, I thought I had just gotten a promotion."

"Sorry, Lance, we don't have to be special, just available," she explained, her face earnest, excitement lighting her eyes.

"Available?" he queried.

"Yes, being at the right place at the right time and willing for God to use us."

"Well, I guess I don't mind God using me, if that's what happened. But as far as my being at the right place at the right time, God didn't have anything to do with that. I was the one who decided where I was going." His eyes refused to meet hers directly, but in them she read determination and apprehension.

Stephanie's eyes twinkled, mischief playing in them. "Don't you know the verse, 'The steps of a good man are ordered by the Lord?'"

" A good man, eh? Maybe I'd better end this conversation while I'm ahead. As for this availability business, I still don't understand it, but perhaps someday we can talk about it again. Meanwhile, what kind of partners are we going to be?" Lance responded deftly, piloting the conversation to safer and more familiar waters.

"What about a limited partnership with an open book policy?" Stephanie was delighted for the opportunity to use something she had learned at the university.

"I'll get my attorney to draw up the agreement." Glancing at his watch, Lance slowly rose to his feet as he held out his hand to her.

She took it but lingered another moment on the bench as she looked up into his eyes, searching his face. "This has been the strangest day of my life. I've handed over my future to a man I've just met, yet I'm not even nervous about it."

"Did you have any other choice, Stephanie?"

"No, not an acceptable one," she agreed as she stood.

"Then accept it as if fate smiled on you. This is going to be a good deal for both of us."

"I believe that, but Lance, it isn't fate."

"Oh, yeah, I forgot, I'm an answer to prayer!" He chuckled aloud.

"Don't worry, I won't let you forget!"

"How can I entertain any ulterior motives if you keep reminding me of that?" Lance's teasing nature was never far from the surface.

"That's what I'm counting on to keep you in line."

"It won't be easy, you know. You're very beautiful." He grinned easily but the look in his eyes was so intimate it sent tingles down her spine.

Her face flushed in the early moonlight as she responded lightly, "I bet you say that to all the Hollywood starlets. Aren't we supposed to be beautiful?"

Lance paused midstep and took both her hands in his and looked down for a long moment. "Yes, but your beauty is so different. It has a mysterious quality that intrigues and challenges me to solve it. Will you let me, Stephanie?"

As Stephanie saw the tenderness in his gaze, she felt her heart leap in response. For the first time in her life someone had pierced her independent spirit and touched the woman's heart beneath, setting it aflame.

The staccato ring of the telephone startled Stephanie who was engrossed in pleasant reflection. Once again she sat in the window seat but now night's inky curtain concealed her view. The day's excitement had denied her both sleep and the ability to read the magazine resting in her lap.

She glanced down at the gold watch whose precious gems embedded in its face colored the hours, mutely proclaiming the passage of time. Her grandmother had worn it as a bride, then her mother, and now she wore it and cherished the memories.

A frown furrowed her smooth brow briefly as she saw the hour was late for a casual call. Apprehensively, she approached the phone, remembering other times when late night calls had heralded tragedies.

"Hello, Boulder Bay, Stephanie Haynes speaking."

A deep, slightly slurred voice responded. "Yes, Ms. Haynes. I've called to see if you have reconsidered my offer."

Stephanie paused before answering. The voice though slightly familiar eluded identification. "I beg your pardon. Who is this?"

"You know me. I'm the man who is going to make you rich. What a dynamite team we will make! I liked the way you performed this afternoon." A deep chuckle punctuated his voice as he added, "I'll have to say though, you really fooled old Jarrett."

"Mr. Dalton?" she asked hesitantly, recognition finally dawning.

"Who else? Your benefactor." The slurring of Dalton's speech now seemed ridiculously exaggerated.

"Who else, indeed? It is very late, and we've completed our business."

Dalton delayed his response for a few seconds. "You are mistaken, Ms. Haynes. We've just begun our business. You do business just like me. You took a big gamble this afternoon. At first you kinda riled me, but when I cooled down, I figured out your game. Anyway, it would be better for me and for you if we leave Jarrett out. Say, since you're still up I'll just drive up, and we'll finish this business."

"Our business is finished, Dalton. Let me make myself clear: I will not sell to you on any terms or at any price."

"That's all right, St-Stephanie, I—"

"You bet it is, and that finishes this conversation."

"Wait! I just told you, Sweetheart, I know what your game is and I'm all for it. I'll just come on up and we'll strike a deal and leave Jarrett out of it altogether. . . better for me, better for you."

"Mr. Dalton. . ."

"Jay."

"Mr. Dalton, I don't want to talk to you tonight or any other day or night. I want you to understand. . . ." Stephanie paused slightly before continuing. "I'm not selling to you or anyone."

A low chuckle filled her ear. "Now that's one bill of goods I won't buy. You've got to do business with me. I was willing to bargain, but you've pushed me too far now."

"Fine. If I were you I wouldn't bargain either. In fact you should just withdraw your offer." Stephanie's voice dropped softly, and she spoke much as she would to a small child she hoped to convince. Dalton's altered speech pattern alarmed her, but his threat to arrive on her doorstep in the middle of the night galvanized her into action.

Cool, common sense now replaced her former irritation with the man as she continued, her voice honeyed. "Jay, it's late and I'm exhausted, besides I really meant it I've decided not to sell, so you would be wasting a trip. Now you wouldn't want to waste a drive up here, would you?"

"But I was gonna offer you three million dollars! Wha-what about that, and you won't even have to give old

Jarrett part of it." He chuckled. "Guess you could use all that dough, eh? I'll be right on out."

"No!" Stephanie answered, more sharply than she intended, panic teasing her composure. Then with a deep breath she said softly, in what she hoped was a persuasive voice, "Not tonight, Jay. Come tomorrow. I'm just too tired to think tonight. I'll explain all about it, and we can talk when we're both fresh."

"You really don't want me to come tonight? Not even for three million dollars? Why, I've got my check all made out."

"No, I'm really too tired. And besides, we can't go behind Mr. Jarrett's back, that's illegal," she reasoned.

"You just leave Jarrett to me. He'll do anything I say, if he knows what's good for him," Dalton threatened.

"Well, Jay, since I don't feel comfortable about dealing like that, maybe you'd better talk to Howard first and make it right before you come out," Stephanie hedged, praying he would forget the conversation come morning.

"Well, all right, but I'm telling you Jarrett will agree to anything I say. But if you're too tired I'll see you at ten in the morning at your place."

"Sure, that will be fine," Stephanie reluctantly agreed, then added, "but I'm still not promising you anything, Jay. You understand that, don't you?"

"Little lady, you are going to sell to me. See you in the morning, Ms. Stephanie Haynes." His answer, brisk and confident, now without a trace of his former slur, sent shivers up and down Stephanie's spine.

She slowly replaced the receiver in its cradle and, with arms crossed, leaned against the wall for a moment. Then with a long sigh of relief, she made her way down the hall and up the stairs to her room, wondering all the while if this latest turn of events in her day would allow her to sleep at all.

Kneeling before her bed, she thanked her Heavenly Father for His miraculous answer to her prayer for assistance. A smile teased the corner of her mouth as she observed that God's answer to her dilemma had certainly come wrapped in a handsome package. Then sleep met her full force, fear and worry swallowed up in the victory of resolution.

five

Stephanie hummed a quiet tune and hugged herself as she watched the golden streaks of dawn pierce the eastern sky, heralding the dawn of a new day. Sometime during the evening hours with Lance, her worry had eased. Facing the future and deciding to take the risk to fight for her dream had lifted the fog of indecision that had enveloped her.

Eager to get on with her plans, Stephanie had worked during the pre-dawn hours preparing financial statements and renovation lists for Lance. With the whole plan down in black and white, she discovered her financial needs were not as great as she had feared. Martha's assumption had been correct. Her main need was time, and Lance would buy that for her.

If the inn ran with a capacity crowd for six months out of the year, it would carry itself with some profit. With guest houses in use and snaring some of the ski tourism, the prospects for Boulder Bay looked as rosy as the eastern sky.

Moving toward the porch's ornate spindled railing, Stephanie leaned against a column. She turned her head toward the horizon to watch, entranced in the beauty. Breathing deeply of the fragrant sea air, she said aloud, "What a difference a day makes. Yesterday seemed so hopeless and today—yes, today so filled with hope. Oh, God, how could I ever doubt Your goodness and loving care?"

So immersed was Stephanie in the beauty before her that she failed to hear the creaking of the old door or see Martha step quietly onto the porch. She jumped and turned wide, questioning eyes when Martha asked, "What was that you were saying, girl?"

Stephanie smiled sheepishly. "Didn't know I was talking out loud."

"Well, girl, you're sure up bright and early—is it good news or bad that's got you up and out?" Martha asked, her face creasing with concern as she searched the younger girl's face for an answer.

Spontaneously, Stephanie grabbed Martha and danced her around the porch. "That's what I was talking about when you startled me, Martha. I was thanking our good Lord for His miraculous blessings."

"Good news, I. . .I ga. . .gather," she stammered as she struggled to gain her composure. "Now you leave me be, Stephanie, I'm too old for such shenanigans. Besides, are you going to tell me all about it before I explode? John and me went to bed while that nice Mr. Donovan was still here."

"How did you know it was Lance?"

"Er. . .I just. . .," the old woman dropped her eyes in embarrassment. Then gaining her usual aplomb, she lifted her head and looked steadily into Stephanie's eyes.

"I could tell you that I had an errand out at the spring house about the time you and he took your walk, but that wouldn't exactly be the whole truth. You see, I wanted to size him up and to make sure you'd be all right. I didn't see who it was when he came. I can tell you right now it was quite a surprise when I saw who you were with and all so friendly like. Guess 'twas a little presumptuous of me, just being an employee and all, but seeing's we were so worried about you, I just thought to ease our minds a bit."

"Presumptuous?" Stephanie stepped back and looked at the older woman, her eyes bright with grateful tears. "Only if love is. You and John are the only family I have—your love and care my anchor."

The creases of concern that had bound the older face relaxed, and the beauty etched by a lifetime of loving responses took control. "Stephanie. . ." Martha could go no further. A slender hand, its skin like fine parchment, reached down and picked up the corner of her snow-white apron as a tear escaped. "I told you yesterday, you're the child we couldn't have. Nothing in this world could mean as much to me and John as caring for you."

"I know that now, but I only realized it yesterday. I had felt so guilty taking advantage of you. But now it looks as if we can go on with our plans, and you can get the pay you so deserve."

"You don't say, now." Martha narrowed her eyes and cocked her head to one side. "You must've had some really good news. Come on in the kitchen and eat while you tell me and John all about these miraculous happenings."

"I'll take you up on that. I'm hungry as a bear."

"All that dancing 'round, I'll wager. Anyway, you surely sound different from yesterday."

"Oh, Martha. Everything is different today!" Stephanie said, closing the front door on the bright orange orb peeping over the eastern horizon.

Breakfast proved to be a celebration feast. The three lingered over the meal as Stephanie shared each detail of her new plans. The previous day she had told them only that she had turned Dalton's offer down and was considering an alternative. Her agitation after the meeting with Dalton had been so evident that Martha and John had not pressed her for more information.

"Stephanie, it sounds too good to be true, and if I wasn't a believer in the goodness of our God, I'd plumb be scared." Martha remarked as John nodded his head silently beside her.

Stephanie looked at him and smiled. He, too, was tall and wiry, with blue eyes that could be piercing or warm and lively as the occasion warranted.

"What do you think, John? Martha and I have done all the talking."

"It sounds like just the answer you've been searching for. The only thing is. . .," he hesitated, uncomfortable in the new role of advisor.

"Go on, John. She wants to know what we think," Martha encouraged proudly.

"I don't like that telephone call you got from Dalton last night. He might show up around here and cause trouble."

Stephanie breathed a sigh of relief, "No, I don't think we'll have to worry. I feel sure he was in his cups too much to remember he even called. Anyway, he's too shrewd a businessman to act the way he did last night when he's sober. Is that the only thing that's bothering you?"

"I've got to admit I would feel better about the whole thing if I'd joined Martha at the spring house and got a look-see at your Mr. Lancelot."

"Lancelot Donovan," Stephanie smilingly corrected. "You did. When he brought me back to the house yesterday morning."

"I wasn't looking at him, young lady. I saw him, but I

wasn't 'looking' at him, if you know what I mean."

Stephanie laughed, "You mean, look him over! Martha, were you surprised when you saw that it was Lance?"

Martha's Mona Lisa smile revealed more than her words, "Not too much."

Stephanie cocked an inquisitive eyebrow at her, but before Martha could respond, the doorbell rang.

A few moments later John ushered in Lance, and soon he was devouring the last remnants of breakfast. By the time the final muffin was gone, Lance had completely charmed the couple. He dispelled any lingering doubts in John's mind by inviting him for a tour of the property to assess the repairs and improvements while the women cleaned up the kitchen.

Stephanie wrinkled her brow, her ready retort aborted when he turned to her, smiling with a strange intimacy that stirred her to her bones. "And then, young lady, you're mine for the rest of the day, understand?"

She nodded her head slowly, mesmerized by his clear, blue eyes. Her heart pounded in furious response.

The two women worked efficiently and silently, both lost in their own thoughts. Stephanie tried to think ahead to the plans she needed to discuss with Lance, but a curious joy that she couldn't explain kept drawing her to introspection.

Stephanie had been on tenterhooks since her mother's death. Tension from all the new and difficult decisions had intensified during the last few days. From her adventures in the cove the previous morning to her confrontation in Jarrett's office, Stephanie had felt every emotion from fear to anger.

Truly that must explain her current euphoria—just plain

old relief—and yet she hadn't felt this curious feeling before breakfast. No, if she were candid with herself, she'd have to admit that the strange sensation arrived shortly after her front doorbell rang—at the exact moment she had encountered the vivid blue of Lancelot Donovan's eyes.

Stephanie stooped to put the bread tins she had just dried into a lower cabinet, glad for the movement to cover the sudden flush tinting her face.

"Why, Stephanie, those pans belong up here. You must be wool gathering," Martha exclaimed. Modifying her tone when she saw Stephanie's face, the older woman added, "And I'd say you've got a right to—there's a lot to think on, all these goings on in the last twenty-four hours."

"Oh, Martha, I'm afraid it's more than wool gathering. The excitement of the past two days seems to have given me butterflies. It just disgusts me. I'm always so cool and collected. I guess keeping Boulder Bay meant more to me than I realized."

"Boulder Bay, hmm?" Martha asked.

Stephanie flushed and lifted an inquisitive eyebrow. "What's that 'hmm' about?"

"Just hmm. That's all."

"No, that's not all. It was steeped in meaning. You might as well be out with it. You will anyway," Stephanie laughingly persisted.

Martha cut her eyes toward Stephanie and said over her shoulder, "Maybe it's Boulder Bay and maybe it's not."

"I'm just relieved, that's all," Stephanie insisted.

"Yup!" Martha's noncommittal answer came brisk and short.

"Why shouldn't I feel relief?"

"You should and probably do, but butterflies don't mean

relief. They mean something else."

"What?" Stephanie frowned.

"Anticipation. Butterflies mean anticipation."

"I guess that's right. I have relieved anticipation!"

"Humph!" snorted Martha.

"My dear lady," Stephanie urged, this time in a serious vein, "will you speak your mind? I *want* you to."

"You're surely relieved, girl, and I know you're excited about the help you'll be getting, but I'm more a mind to attribute the butterflies to the helper than to the help."

"You mean Lance?"

Martha responded with a firm nod of her head. "That's exactly what I mean."

"Martha, you're an incorrigible matchmaker! I have known Lance Donovan less than twenty-four hours. Don't you think you're a little premature?"

The older woman paused before answering. "Tell me this: When did your butterflies arrive? Before or after the doorbell?"

Stephanie's eyebrows shot up in shocked amazement, but before she could answer, the doorbell rang again, ending their lively exchange.

The two women stared at each other and simultaneously looked at the wall clock. It chimed ten times before Stephanie started toward the door.

"I guess I was wrong. Dalton must've remembered. I'll face the music," she sighed.

Stephanie glanced down at her bare feet and brief denim shorts topped with a Boulder Bay T-shirt. She paused to glance in the mirror and gathered her abundant locks into a barrette.

"You're prompt, Mr. Dalton. Please come in. We can

talk in the parlor."

The swarthy, dark-haired man had shed his business suit in favor of a kelly golfing shirt and pale yellow, close-fitting trousers which accented his deep tan and muscular physique.

Stephanie had to admit that he was an attractive man in an overpowering way. He flashed a vivid smile beneath a dark, neatly trimmed mustache, and his manner proved impeccably charming as he entered the room with a slight swagger. His actions last night had not dampened his confidence; he appeared completely at ease.

Stephanie's courage faltered.

"Please be seated, Mr. Dalton," she directed with an outward poise that belied her thumping heart. She became acutely aware of her shorts and shirt as Jay Dalton's deliberate gaze took her in from head to toe.

An appreciative smile began at one corner of his mouth and spread to a wide, full grin. "Can it be possible? You're lovelier than I remembered."

"Thank you, Mr. Dalton—"

"Jay," he corrected.

"Jay, but I don't believe the way I look has any bearing on our business."

"You're wrong. It makes it much more pleasant, and I have to confess my only weakness is beautiful women. You might say, I'm putty in their hands. You see, I will enjoy doing business more, but you will have the advantage," his eyes slid over her once more as he nodded. "A decided advantage."

The man's boldness stirred a cauldron of anger within Stephanie, setting her countenance in disgust. "Who I am or how I look will not affect our business, Mr. Dalton," she replied coldly.

She fought to control her anger as she softened her tone, realizing the potential danger in her situation. Jay Dalton was a powerful man, perhaps with unsavory connections. "Jay," she amended, "I tried to explain last evening, but you seemed, uh. . .preoccupied."

He smiled knowingly, acknowledging nothing, "Not too preoccupied to remember what you said or to understand the game you're playing. Stephanie, let's get to the bottom line. I intend to have Boulder Bay, one way or the other. I know you need the money, and I'd rather you have it than the bank. Just how much will it take to satisfy you?" The dazzling smile parted the dark face once again, but the eyes remained cold and calculating.

"Not anything you have. Boulder Bay is not for sale."

A humorless laugh interrupted her, "Anything has its price. Tell me what's yours. Let's quit playing games and finish our business."

Her eyes rounded in amazement, and she paused before replying. "I wish I could make you understand, Mr. Dalton. You can't buy Boulder Bay."

"Because you don't approve of what you think my plans are for it?"

A slow smile softened Stephanie's face and warmth touched her eyes. "I don't expect you to understand, and I can't explain it any better than I did yesterday. If I aided you in doing something which violates my convictions, then all the money in the world couldn't compensate for it. What price can even you put on peace of mind, Jay?"

He stared back at her, incredulity written on his face, yet his eyes for an instant were unguarded, warmed by a puzzled admiration. Then his hooded eyes grew cold and hard as if rejecting what he'd recognized. "Ms. Haynes, I've found the only way to assure my peace of mind is to buy it."

"That's unfortunate, Jay Dalton, for if having Boulder Bay is important to your peace of mind, you'll lose out. I won't sell to you, now or ever."

Anger flared briefly in the cold, ebony eyes, and he clenched his jaw, but quickly had himself under control. In a gentle, persuasive voice, he remarked, "This is a strange turn of events. Yesterday you seemed willing until I refused to agree to your ridiculous stipulation. Took me a few hours to realize it was a ploy. I think you're still playing."

Stephanie threw up her hands in exasperation and walked away from her visitor to the window. She looked out over the rolling lawn. The grass, a lush green, extended to a rock ledge that plunged straight to the breakers below.

"It's easy to see why you're so persistent," she remarked without facing him. "This is a place of resplendent beauty and the only gem of privately owned property on this section of the coast. A valuable investment for whatever your plans may be. My reasons for turning you down yesterday haven't changed, but my circumstances have. I don't have to sell now."

"You're mistaken. You have to sell it—to me."

Stephanie whirled around, patience at an end and an angry retort on her lips. "That's—"

The words hung in mid-air as she collided, face to chest, with the bright green shirt. The pungent herbal fragrance of Jay Dalton's aftershave overpowered her. He had moved silently from his seat and now stood squarely boxing her in. Stephanie retreated. With her back pressed against the window, she held her head high, eyes questioning, but her stomach churned with alarm.

Dalton smiled darkly, enjoying his advantage, and crooned softly, "Are you ready to talk business or play games?"

"I'm...I'm...," Stephanie stammered hesitantly. Then squaring her shoulders, she threw her head back and looked him squarely in the eye. They stood so for a moment, eyes locked in combat, piercing black ones against icy blue.

From across the room a deep-timbred voice spoke with calm authority. "Mr. Dalton, I believe my partner has spoken for both of us. Boulder Bay is not for sale."

Jay Dalton whirled, astonishment written on his craggy features. Stephanie slipped quickly from her cornered position.

"Who are you, and why are you interfering?"

"I'm Lance Donovan, movie producer and business partner with Stephanie Haynes. I have been informed of your offer, and we are in complete agreement. No sale." Lance spoke amiably as he strolled across the room toward Stephanie. With three long strides, he reached her and put a possessive arm around her shoulders, offering a haven of protection.

He cast a reassuring smile at Stephanie and added, "I wholeheartedly agree with you, Dalton. She is an enchanting creature, but she's more than that. She knows what she wants and can't be swayed. Admirable quality, don't you think?"

Jay Dalton recovered his composure more rapidly than Stephanie and looked Lance steadily in the eyes. A charged message coursed between them as he silently acknowledged the challenge in Lance's soft statement.

With an abrupt change in tactics he spoke in a concilia-tory tone as he turned to Stephanie. "I guess I owe you an apology, Ms. Haynes. In my business, bluff is the name of the game. I sincerely thought you were holding out for more money."

He paused and once again looked Lance squarely in the eye, this time issuing his own challenge to the younger man. "Are you Ms. Haynes' social secretary as well as her partner? I had intended to invite her to dinner this evening. Surely she doesn't have to work night and day."

"No, but she's spending the evening with me. In fact, from now on she'll be spending all her free time with me. Tonight we're going out to dinner. Could you recommend a good restaurant, some place extra special? You know I'm new to the area."

Stephanie remained silent, her eyes round in disbelief as Dalton raised his eyebrows in surprise, then threw his head back and laughed heartily.

"Donovan, you're all right. Why don't both you and Ms. Haynes be my guests at the yacht club? It's the best place in town, and you can only dine there if you're with a member."

"Thank you, but no. Tell me, Dalton, would you want to share the attention of this lovely lady if you were me?"

"No, but I thought I'd try anyway. I don't give up easily," he responded lightly and, turning his head toward Stephanie, he added with a pleasant smile, "I meant what I said. You are a lovely lady, and I'd enjoy doing business with you. You have my number if you change your mind."

"She won't," Lance interrupted.

Jay Dalton's smile broadened, and he shifted his gaze

toward Lance. "Don't be too sure. I intend to have Boulder Bay, and I always get what I want."

Stephanie shivered as she looked from one man to the other. Dalton's smile did not hide the determination his voice conveyed.

Lance tilted his head to one side and stroked his chin before replying softly, "But you have never wanted anything that was mine before." The warm blue of his eyes had turned to steel gray.

Stephanie found her voice. "Lance is quite right, Mr. Dalton. I won't be changing my mind. I appreciate your interest and am sorry we've taken up so much of your time. I know that you, as we, have a busy morning ahead. Therefore, I won't detain you any longer."

"Yes, I need to be going. Never mind showing me out," he responded as Stephanie walked toward the door. "I know the way. Until later, have a pleasant evening."

Stephanie let out a long sigh when she heard the front door close. "Thank you, Lance. It was very kind of you to intercede like that. But I'm afraid you gave Dalton the wrong idea about us."

"How's that?"

"That somehow you are in charge of my life."

"In a way I am."

"We are partners—business partners."

"I know that. So what's the problem?"

"Well, you made him think. . ."

"Think what?"

"You know."

"Know what?"

"That you had control of other parts of my life."

"So?"

"I don't want him to think that."

"Think what?"

"That you have any other interest in me than business." Stephanie's voice edged with impatience.

"But I do."

"Now, Lancelot Donovan!"

"Honorable. Completely honorable," Lance responded with a look of mock horror on his face.

"Lance, please be serious."

"I am."

"Then let me be serious. I appreciate your help this morning—more than I could tell you—but I don't want anyone, including Jay Dalton, to think that there's anything about our relationship that's not above board."

"He doesn't. Unless the man is totally blind and without a smidgen of understanding, he knows you are a woman of principle. Your whole countenance glows with innocence. Why do you think he was giving you such a hard time? He thought you'd be easy to intimidate," Lance explained.

"Well, I'm not easily intimidated, and I hope you're right about his understanding," came Stephanie's doubtful reply.

"Take it from a man of the world. Who you are shows. That's why I'm here, to protect you."

"I thought you were interested in a business deal."

Lance paused and looked at her, all traces of his lighthearted teasing gone, "I was, but suddenly I find that each time I look at you I forget about our business. I meant it when I told Dalton to forget seeing you. I plan to take up all your time. You see, I'm going to marry you some day, Stephanie Haynes."

Words of protest died on Stephanie's lips as she encountered the tender resoluteness in the vivid blue eyes that held hers. Only her heart thundered an utterance.

six

Stephanie barely noticed when spring gave way to summer. After Lance assessed the needs and potential of Boulder Bay, he made swift plans and began immediate execution of them. He had a movie to get under production, and the major improvements had to be completed before he could begin. Stephanie shared his determination, eager to prove the confidence he had in her.

They saw each other often but had no time to talk intimately again, nor did Lance seem inclined to elaborate on his earlier, startling statement. Warm friendship and respect permeated their relationship.

Lance's uncanny business sense discovered potential revenue-producing projects that Stephanie had either overlooked or had lacked the money to pursue. He mapped out the improvements he wanted and gave Stephanie a budget to work from. Her large, blue eyes widened in disbelief when she saw the size of it. She protested vehemently.

He silenced her with his reasonable explanation that it takes money to make money. His eagerness to release the untapped potential of the property knew no bounds. Stephanie, cautious by necessity and by nature, felt anxious at first, but gradually her anxiety eased as she caught Lance's vision. Determined to contribute her part, she threw herself wholeheartedly into getting the best job done the most economically.

Following Lance's master plan to the smallest detail, she supervised the project and developed skills of bargaining and supervision that she hadn't known she possessed. The workmen came early, but they always found Stephanie there before them. However late they left, she was still busy, planning and inspecting their work. The inn reached its last stages of completion just as the date for Lance's production approached.

Stephanie felt relieved that business had left little time for intimate conversation. Disturbing questions hammered at her mind, but she ignored them, glad she could throw her heart into the work at hand and fall exhausted into bed at night. She told herself a thousand times that Lance had been teasing and the sheer jubilance she felt was the result of seeing her dream of Boulder Bay come alive before her eyes.

Like the proverbial Phoenix rising from the ashes, the whole place took on a new dimension. Where it had been a large, comfortable, rambling house, it now resided in a gown of splendor. The crew painted the old, white clapboards a pastel blue and repaired and replaced the ornate Victorian trim, painting it a dazzling white.

Craftsmen cleaned the stained glass windows, restoring them to their original beauty. Antiques and authentic reproductions furnished the rooms, adding irresistible charm. Workmen replaced old plumbing and modernized the kitchen with every convenience needed for serving capacity crowds. A garden room was added to enlarge the dining facilities, and a large grand piano sat in regal splendor in one corner.

Because of Martha's culinary artistry, Lance decided to establish the inn as a gourmet paradise, pulling in local diners as well as tourist and inn guests. His aim: an expensive night of epicurean delight in an elegant atmosphere topped off with good entertainment.

He turned the coach house into a coffee shop, equipping it with a fireplace built from boulders found on the property. From the terrace, diners could overlook the new pool and tennis courts.

Professional landscapers added gardens and rock pathways along the deserted bluff above the rugged coast, but Stephanie's private cove was fenced off. As if by unspoken agreement, Lance let it remain as it was, Stephanie's private sanctuary.

Where the coast curved gently inward to form a protected inlet, they built a dock and boathouse. Soon Stephanie's forty-foot sloop, *Carefree*, sat anchored in readiness. Her teak deck sparkled, cleaned and refurbished by a part-time college crew, eagerly awaiting their first customer to charter her for an hour, day, or week.

As the final weeks approached, Stephanie and Lance saw less and less of one another, each absorbed with the work at hand. Even so their friendship strengthened with each passing day; they were two people who had deep respect for one another and shared a common goal.

Martha had been too busy to engage in her matchmaking pursuits, but she'd noticed Stephanie's growing radiance and caught Lance's lingering glance when Stephanie walked away from him. She smiled knowingly; a business venture alone couldn't light up a woman's eyes like that. Martha told John as much, adding that she could rest easy if Stephanie had a man like Lance to look after her.

Before Stephanie was quite prepared, summer waned and a hint of fall teased the air. She redoubled her efforts and worked even longer hours. When darkness swallowed up the long twilight shadows, she worked on her accounts in the light of an old seaman's lamp on her small rosewood desk.

The size of the invoices and payroll astounded her, but when she checked her budget, it remained well below Lance's estimate. Her excitement grew. Already there was a sizable income from the chartering of *Carefree*. The college crew had been so excited about the adventure that they had taken care of the advertising. Demand had exceeded the number of trips they could run.

It was Lance who had realized the charter potential of Stephanie's sloop, but it was her idea to channel the energy and enthusiasm for sailing of the local young people. The success was just another example of how well Lance and Stephanie worked together.

Once she had caught Lance's vision for Boulder Bay, Stephanie knew that he was right. She determined to bring that vision to reality, but substantially under the budget. Now it looked as if she would have a sizable amount to give back to Lance on completion of the project.

After the first month, he had not looked at the books with her. At first the responsibility he had entrusted her with worried her, but now it gave her a sense of satisfaction.

When refurbishing the cottages got under way, Lance took a personal interest in them. Without explanation, he enlarged one to include an office, extra bedroom, kitchen, and solarium. Since it was the cottage nearest the sea, it seemed reasonable to Stephanie that it should be enhanced for a honeymoon cottage, and Lance's personal involvement in it puzzled her.

Shortly before its completion, Lance arrived late one

afternoon in a bright red truck, loaded with his personal belongings. Stephanie, brown as a berry from her busy weeks outdoors, met him and raised an inquisitive brow.

The bright afternoon sun caught the merry lights flashing in Lance's vivid blue eyes. One side of his mouth turned up in a lopsided grin. "I can't stand being so far away from you, so I'm moving in."

Stephanie smiled, not believing him. "Sure you are."

"If you won't marry me, what choice do I have?" he countered, attempting a pitiful countenance.

"You poor little lamb," she laughed as she impulsively reached up and patted his cheek. "Seriously, what are you doing?"

"Just like I told you—moving in. I can't go on living without seeing that beautiful face every day," he responded, putting his hand over his heart in mock seriousness. "Oh, to see those beautiful eyes across the breakfast table from me every morning—it must be thus or I die."

"Lance, you're incorrigible," Stephanie laughed.

"Yeh, but ain't I fun?" he quipped, his face alight with laughter.

"You still haven't answered my question. What are you doing?" she insisted.

"Moving in."

Stephanie's smile faded and she looked at him, the question in her eyes turning them dark and wary.

Lance stepped over to her and, taking her chin in his hand, tilted her face upward to his. He was standing so close to her that she could see the spidery fine laughter lines around his eyes and hear his steady breathing.

Lance bent his head and kissed her lightly on her upturned lips. "The cottage, Sweetheart. The cottage. I fixed it up for me. It's perfect. Save me time, rent, and the best thing of all—I *can* have breakfast with you every morning." He smiled gently, reassuringly at her, then with an impish grin added, "Course, to be honest—Martha's cooking had a great deal to do with my decision. She does cook breakfast every morning, doesn't she?"

Stephanie stepped back from his kiss as if an electrical current had coursed through her body. Embarrassment and relief flushed her face. "I'm sure. . . ." she stammered, dropping her eyes.

He lifted her chin again, "You're sure, what?"

"That Martha'll be glad to have you!" she finished, her voice shrill in her ears.

He stepped even closer, never releasing her chin. Her head came to just below his shoulder, and she could see the even rise and fall of his broad, muscular chest. Lance tilted her head farther back, forcing her to meet his eyes. "And what about Miss.Stephanie Haynes? How does she feel about it?"

The look in his eyes, his very nearness, returned the disturbing emotions that she had pushed away all summer. How could she deny the joy, desire, and even terror that he stirred within her? Did she want him to stay at Boulder Bay where she could see him every day, hear his voice, see the way the sun caught the copper glint in his hair, feel the warmth of his eyes as intimate as an embrace when they rested on her?

The truth. He wanted the truth, but how could she tell him? It was what she wanted, God help her, with all her heart. Instead she closed her eyes, wrinkled her nose, and remarked with as much nonchalance as she could muster, "I might be able to put up with you, Mr. Donovan—if you'll behave yourself."

His smile broadened as he released her. "I knew you'd see it my way, my dear. I'll do my best to behave, but it won't be easy. You'd better be thankful we have more work to do than hours to finish it, 'cause otherwise you might prove to be a fatal distraction, and I'd be tempted to break my word to you—sweep you off your feet and look for a preacher. . ."

"Lance. . . ." she began, trying to look stern.

"No, no, I know we're not ready for that yet—neither of us. I just said it would be tempting." The laughter in his eyes muted and he added, his tone softly serious, "You're a delicious woman, Stephanie Haynes, like none other I've ever met. Someday I'll tell you just how much you mean to me; but right now, we've dragons to slay."

"Dragons?" she asked puzzled.

"Jay Dalton. Has he approached you again about Boulder Bay?"

"No, why?"

"Several evenings lately the workmen said they've seen him parked up on the bluff watching the progress down here. I feel sure that he will make another offer. He doesn't give up easily, and I want to know how you feel about it. The place is still yours, and if you decide you want to sell, it's okay."

"I still feel the same. Why, Lance? Has there been some change in your financial status? Do you need your money back?"

"No, I just wanted to be sure that you still feel the same."

"I do. I couldn't sell it to him for what he wants to do with it, but aside from that, seeing it transformed like this— why it exceeds my wildest dreams. The only worry I have is how soon you will get a profitable return on your investment. You've spent a lot more money than I had anticipated. The improvements have been so much more elaborate than I had envisioned."

"It will take longer to pay for the improvements, but in the long run your revenue producing potential is much greater. Using the inn as a location for the film will be a windfall for me. It will cost the film less, and we will be making a profit at the same time. By enlarging the facilities, we can open the inn up to other guests while we are filming and that will be a drawing card."

"How do you plan to get the word out?" Stephanie questioned, marveling at Lance's innovative ideas.

"News releases. Hollywood and the surrounding area are interested in the movie project, so we'll just casually include our plans for using this place as a location."

"You're pretty sharp, Lance Donovan."

"Did you ever have any doubts about that?" he quipped.

She chuckled. "Well, I did have a moment or two at the beginning, if you recall."

Lance threw back his head and laughed. "Especially about my proposition. Boy, did you get your dander up about that. Did I ever tell you how beautiful you are when you're angry? You're like fire and ice—absolutely breathtaking."

"Lance, you're impossible!"

"No, I'm an artist, among all my other wonderful attributes. I'm an expert on beauty—and I can tell you something else, I can read emotion."

Stephanie shot him a quick look and warned, "Be careful that you don't read too much into them. You might get hurt."

His gaze was steady as it met hers. "Don't worry. I won't. Anyway the time's not right yet. By the way, would you happen to have any leftovers for a homeless man?"

"Leftovers?" she responded, her brow wrinkled.

He grinned at her, "Yeh, the kitchen kind. I couldn't eat, thinking about Martha's cooking just waiting for me."

"You're in luck. There's soup and salad in the kitchen and a strawberry pie in the oven. Come on, hungry man, let's feed you before you suffer the vapors."

He bent in a mock bow and lifted her hand to his lips, murmuring, "Lead on, fair maiden, and sit thee before me or I perish."

After an ample meal, Lance unloaded his belongings with Stephanie's help. Martha had sent over cookies and a large pitcher of lemonade, and the two had just sat down on the large porch overlooking the sea when a smart, yellow sports car drove up the drive and stopped outside. Stephanie watched the immaculate brunette walk hurriedly up the rock walk and recognized her just before she reached the door.

"Hello, Abigail," Stephanie called from the porch."Just follow the walk on around. We're here on the porch. Come have a glass of lemonade." Lance looked at Stephanie questioningly and she replied softly, "Abigail, Mr. Jarrett's secretary."

He rose from his chair when she opened the door, and smilingly acknowledged the brief introduction.

Abigail smiled shyly, "I hate to interrupt you. . ."

"You're not interrupting anything, Abigail. I'm glad to see you," Stephanie responded, realizing she felt genuinely glad to see the young woman. "I told you to come out anytime, you know."

"Yes, thank you, I remembered. That's one of the reasons why I'm here. I'm on my way back home."

"A visit?" Lance questioned.

Tears filled the somber, dark eyes. "No, to stay. I've lost my job."

"What happened, Abigail?" Stephanie asked, concern clouding the bright blue of her eyes.

"Do you remember the conversation we had before you went in to see Mr. Jarrett?"

"About your job?"

"No, about what Mr. Dalton wanted to do with your place."

"Yes."

"That started me to thinking. The fact that your convictions were so strong you'd risk losing your place rather than compromise made an impression on me. I began to question what went on in the office. Some things happened, some business deals that—well, I won't elaborate. I'll just say I couldn't in good conscience participate in them. Mr. Jarrett told me to do it or to leave; so I left."

"I'm sure that you did the right thing, and you'll be better off for it," Stephanie soothed.

A wan smile appeared briefly, lifting Abigail's countenance. "It's rather embarrassing for me. Everyone will ask questions, and there's no telling what Mr. Jarrett will tell them. You're the only two I've talked to, and the only reason I've come to you is to warn you. I've really struggled with this—trying to evaluate if I should betray what I heard while in the employ of Mr. Jarrett."

"Something that affects Stephanie, Abigail?" Lance asked. Stephanie could see him tense beneath his warm hospitable stance.

"To both of you. You are her business associate, aren't you?"

"Yes. Now tell us." Lance responded, his voice edged with urgency.

"It's Dalton. He and Jarrett were talking. He's determined to get your place. When you paid off the bank, and he realized that hope of a default was gone, he went into a rage. About a week ago he came back, and I heard him tell Jarrett that he'd found a way, and it would be only a matter of time before Boulder Bay was his. He laughed and said that it had worked out better for him anyway; the improvements were superb, and he'd gotten all the benefit of your time and expertise without having to pay for it."

"Abigail, how did he say he was going to accomplish this?" Lance asked.

"He didn't. He just said there were more roads to Rome than one and something about his trip to Las Vegas. Then they noticed the door was ajar and closed it. That's all I could hear."

"Lance, what could he mean?" Stephanie asked, her face creased with worry.

"Don't let it worry you, honey. He's just blowing off steam."

"I don't think he was," Abigail disputed with a shake of her head. "They talked a long time after that, and he was too jubilant not to have a solution."

"I can't think of anything he can do to us, can you, Lance?" Stephanie puzzled.

"Nope, not if you've been paying the bills on time," Lance replied with a reassuring wink, but not before Stephanie could see a vestige of doubt in his usually confident eyes.

"By the way, Abigail. Speaking of paying the bills, how would you like a job here with us?" Lance continued.

Stephanie looked from Lance to Abigail and back again questioningly.

"Production is about to start, and I need a good secretary," he explained. "Stephanie will be involved in the picture soon and could use some administrative help running the lodge and inn. What do you say, Steph?"

"You know what you need better than I do, Lance. I'm sure Abigail would make you an efficient secretary," Stephanie answered stiffly.

"It's not me that I'm thinking of. I know you. You won't get anyone to help you. I don't want my ingenue to look tired and haggard." He looked at her, mild pleading in his eyes.

Relieved, she smiled her assent and asked, "Can we afford it?"

"Sure we can. Taking care of you is my first priority." Once more the message in his vivid blue eyes sent chills of fear and delight straight to Stephanie's heart.

The three quickly worked out the details of Abigail's job. She would live on the premises, taking her room and board as part of her compensation. Her salary was less than it had been at Brown, Jarrett and Jarrett's, but Stephanie suggested profit-sharing options and bonuses that would make up the difference. Soon a happy Abigail unloaded her little sports car, and Boulder Bay had another resident.

seven

Abigail settled into her new job with ease and efficiency, and within a month she proved indispensable to both Lance and Stephanie while garnering a reluctant Martha's affection. John observed her in wary silence, but soon her sincerity and good humor had won him over completely.

The dining room opened with a flourish, and the first week the crowds overflowed. They came to experience a culinary treat and lingered to enjoy the romantic dinner music. Stephanie and Martha opened the coach house and used it as a secondary dining room. Music from the solarium wafted across the pool, and diners sat beneath the stars on the terrace. Each left having experienced an evening of outstanding quality. They told their friends and their friends came. Crowds upon crowds—and they were never disappointed.

Lance was too busy with the final preparations of his film to take an active part in the opening of the restaurant, but Stephanie filled in as needed, sometimes as hostess and sometimes in the kitchen. Every evening, she and Abigail totaled up the receipts, and after only a month, she saw the wisdom of Lance's investment in Martha's culinary genius. The dining room proved an unqualified success, and thanks to Abigail's attention to careful shopping, it promised to be a very profitable endeavor.

Each night, Stephanie fell into bed past midnight in happy exhaustion. She had yet to take a meal in the dining hall, preferring to catch a bite in the kitchen with Abigail and Lance.

One afternoon, Stephanie strolled over to Lance's bungalow to see how it looked after he had furnished and decorated it. Her time had been so involved at the main inn that she had left the completion of the cottages to Lance and Abigail.

She heard a deep baritone voice singing gustily as she approached the porch facing the ocean. A warm smile parted her face when she recognized Lance's voice singing one of the old love songs played the night before. She joined her sweet lilting soprano with his, and they finished the chorus together.

He rose from his seat on the porch when he saw her, delight flaring in his eyes. Meeting her at the door, he opened it and motioned her in. "Wow, we ought to be in show biz—the Dynamo Duo. Do you reckon we could get a job at Boulder Inn?"

"I don't know. I think we ought to practice, don't you?"

"I've been for that from the beginning." His eyes held hers. "Give me a kiss—"

"To build a dream on," she chimed in, her eyes soft and shining. Happiness bubbled inside her.

Suddenly the singing died as she looked up into his vivid blue eyes. The mirth in them faded, exchanged for something undefinable that left her breathless.

Lance moved closer and without taking his eyes from hers, he lifted her hand and pressed it to his lips. "Stephanie Haynes, if you look at me like that one more time, I can't vouch for your safety. I was thinking of you while I sang, and then you appeared like a beautiful vision. It's almost more than this love-sick man can stand."

Stephanie's brow wrinkled as she searched his face. Was he teasing her again? His words sounded light, but his eyes betrayed him. She saw apprehension, almost fear in them. But of what? His own emotions? Her response?

She laughed softly, trying to relieve the tension between them. "I bet you say that to all your beautiful female visitors. Never fear, I can take care of myself, but I will watch these expressive eyes. I wouldn't want to tempt you unduly," she lowered her long lashes in a mock apology.

A low chuckle started in Lance's throat and spread to a full laugh, clearing the emotion-charged air.

Stephanie sighed with relief as he remarked, "Well, you little vixen, you wouldn't come in second to Miss Scarlett herself with those fluttering lashes. Yes, ma'am, I've got myself a little actress on my hands."

"Lance, all you talk about is business, business, business, and here I came looking for a break," she teased.

He raised his eyebrows and searched her face, blandly replying, "Where you are concerned, that's the safest subject. By the way, you need to set aside tomorrow afternoon and evening. The camera crew arrives in the morning, and I need to set up your screen test."

"Will it take that long?"

"No, but afterwards I want to take you out to dinner. How about a date?"

"Any place in particular?"

"How about that new place over at Boulder Bay?"

"You mean the dining room or kitchen?"

"The choice dining room table, so put on your best duds. We're dining in style."

"That sounds like fun."

"Time we had some fun, don't you think?"

"Well, yes, I. . . ." Stephanie hesitated, a faint blush tinting her cheeks.

Lance raised an eyebrow, waiting. When she failed to continue, he gently urged, "Any problem?"

A timid smile touched her lips and she finished softly, "Working with you *has* been fun. More fun than I've ever had in my life."

"I'm talking about a different kind of fun, Steph. I mean the strictly 'me and you' kind of fun. Where I can stare at you in the candlelight, with love songs in the background, listen to the sweet sound of your voice as it speaks my name, and afterwards hold your hand while we walk in the moonlight. Nothing to do with our joy of accomplishment this time; just the plain joy of being alone with you." His eyes were soft, and his voice held a gentle intensity as he added, "There's more to life than work."

A lump constricted Stephanie's throat. Lance had opened a floodgate of longing. She turned from him toward the door when she could finally speak and, nodding her head, said simply, "I'll be ready."

The next morning the atmosphere at the inn crackled with excitement. By mid-morning, the first vans and trucks arrived, bringing camera crew and equipment. Then came the wardrobe van and the make-up artists.

Stephanie worked swiftly and efficiently with Abigail to get them settled. By early afternoon, every crew member had his room assignment and had enjoyed a sumptuous lunch, enabling Stephanie to report promptly to the basement production department for her wardrobe and make-up, then on to the filming room.

The morning's activities had kept her too busy for

anxiety to creep in, but now her palms dampened and her heart beat wildly when Lance met her in the narrow hall. His encouraging smile calmed her and, much to her surprise, she thoroughly enjoyed the filming session.

Lance's relaxed instruction brought her through step by step, and when he called an end to the session, she experienced a fleeting moment of disappointment.

Lance's features were animated with controlled excitement. Stephanie raised her eyebrows, tilting her head to one side as she waited for an explanation.

He offered none. With a wave of his hand, he dismissed her, saying nonchalantly, "I think this'll do, kitten. See you at seven!"

Stephanie walked slowly from the room, her small white teeth pulling absentmindedly on her bottom lip. She felt let down. Why? It seemed natural that she should. After all, she'd been working toward this day since early spring. She sighed. What happened to the happy sense of accomplishment? Perhaps the screen test traumatized her more than she realized.

Apprehension knotted her stomach. What if it didn't turn out well? Did it really matter? She didn't want to disappoint Lance, yet she'd never had any desire to be a movie star. She pulled at her lip again. She had enjoyed the screening though.

On down the hall she strolled, head down, deep in thought. With a shrug of her shoulders, she reached out to take the railing of the stairs, her foot paused on the first step. It wasn't her work or her test! It was Lance. He had been so. . .so businesslike with her. Encouraging, accommodating, but that special way he looked at her. It hadn't been there! And she'd missed it. Had she ever missed it!

Stephanie smiled and walked up the stairs. Amused at herself, she acknowledged that by necessity her relationship with Lance would have to change. They would have to put aside the casual atmosphere they had enjoyed all summer or risk a morale and discipline problem on the set. This movie was big business, and Lance was the boss.

Her smile broadened at the thought. This Lance she'd not seen before—one with a controlled energy that commanded respect and response. A competent business mind whose attention remained fixed on the project at hand had replaced the slightly impudent young man with the teasing eyes. The metamorphosis intrigued her, yet she couldn't shake the uneasy feeling in the pit of her stomach. How would this affect their relationship?

For the first time, Stephanie acknowledged her dependence on Lance. Her delicate brows knit together in a frown as her emotions sought safer ground. How could she allow that? Dependency meant enslavement. Hadn't she made that decision a long time ago? Yet her heart refused to listen as the image of Lance's laughing blue eyes danced before her. She hurried up the stairs, breathless in anticipation of the evening ahead.

Stephanie smiled at her reflection. Her hair hung loose to her shoulders in a golden cloud with silver lights. Her long, white dress draped her body. A silver belt clasped her narrow waist, and the silky material lay softly across her small rounded hips in a gentle caress before falling gracefully to the floor.

The vivid white set off Stephanie's sun-bronzed skin, and her eyes, wide with excitement, sparkled like sapphires. Tonight, she wanted to be beautiful. The mirror told her that she was.

So did Lance's eyes. He saw her the moment she left her room. She walked across the open balcony and, pausing, she looked down at him over the ornate rail. Her full, pink lips parted in a half-smile. Then with queenly grace, she slowly descended the curved staircase. She felt the warmth of Lance's approving gaze, and enjoyed the pleasure it stirred inside her. Then their eyes locked and her heart raced. His eyes smoldered a passionate message, and Stephanie saw yet another Lance.

She walked up to him, and he briefly rested his hands on her small, square shoulders. Running his finger tips in a light caress down her arms to her hands, he lifted them and pressed each one to his lips. "You are the most beautiful woman I've ever seen." His voice was husky with emotion.

"You approve?" she dimpled up at him, reveling in this strange new power she possessed.

"I think you could say that," he said with a half smile. "Is it—the dress—new?"

"Yes. Abigail saw it when she was in town and brought it home on approval. I was going to take it back, but when you said you wanted me to get my best duds on, I couldn't resist the temptation."

Tucking her hand inside the curve of his arm, Lance pulled her closer to him, and they walked out the door. "I'm glad you didn't. I've never seen anything to compare with you in that dress."

"Thank you, Sir Lancelot. I aimed to please."

He smiled at her. No words were needed. His eyes burned his appreciation.

The evening continued with the same promise that it

began. From the meal of seafood delicacy to the softly throbbing romantic songs from a bygone year, Stephanie's senses were filled with heady delight.

Later Stephanie couldn't remember what they discussed during dinner. She could only recall Lance's eyes blazing into hers with a message that needed no utterance.

They were enjoying their after-dessert coffee when Lance asked her how she felt about her screen test.

"I really enjoyed it. Although I was nervous at first, before long I forgot about the camera and just enjoyed the experience."

"I thought you did."

A shy smile teased her lip,s and she traced the intricate designs on the damask cloth with her finger, then glancing up at him through her lashes, she added, "I couldn't have done it without you. Your instructions were perfect."

He chuckled, "You just keep believing that, Sweetheart."

She turned her full, wide eyes on him questioningly.

"That you need me," he explained, his mouth curving with tenderness.

She dropped her head, not wanting him to see the response that flamed in her eyes. But he had, and rising, he took her hand and pulled her to her feet. "It's time for that moonlit walk."

The night sky blazed with stars, and a gentle breeze cooled the air. Soft strains of music drifted after them as they strolled across the lawn toward the bluff and the bench they had shared so many months before. Stephanie shivered, partly from the cool night air and partly from the heady excitement of the moment.

Lance stopped and, taking off his coat, draped it around

her and pulled her to him in a gentle, undemanding embrace. Unresisting, she rested her head on his shoulder.

They stood thus for a long moment. Stephanie could hear the beat of his heart, echoing the thundering sea beneath them. The scent of his aftershave teased her nostrils, and the towering strength of his tall, masculine body gave her a quiet sense of security and safety.

She stirred and tried to pull away, suddenly afraid of this haven, her dependence, her need for it.

Lance felt her resistance and tightened his hold. "Don't pull away, Stephanie. I've waited an eternity to hold you like this. Tonight is our night. No other world exists but ours, no others but us; nothing else matters but our love."

Stephanie lifted her head and stared intently into his eyes, longing and fear battling in hers. Her long blond hair, silver in the moonlight, cascaded down her back.

With a low guttural groan, Lance bent his head to hers and kissed the soft, full mouth turned up to him. The kiss lingered. It throbbed with the passion of demand, yet flowing with a tender love that finally ended in a crescendo of victory as two hearts united in spirit while time and space receded. Stephanie forgot her fears. In that moment only Lance existed, the safety of his arms, the power of his kiss, the rivers of delight he sent flowing through her with his love, with his embrace, with his kiss.

Finally, he released her and a knowing smile crinkled his eyes. "Stephanie, I love you, and you love me."

A frown wrinkled her wide, smooth brow, and her eyes looked dark in the bright moonlight. She shook her head and said breathlessly, "Lance, don't push me. The night, the moonlight—it's too romantic to rely on."

He chuckled softly in her ear. "It isn't the moonlight,

darling. It's me and you. We were made for each other. I never believed that was possible before I met you. If you'll tell the truth, you'll have to admit it, Steph." Slipping his arm around her waist, he picked up her hand and, placing it on his heart, laughed. "It's like a herd of wild horses every time you come near me whether it's in the moonlight or broad daylight."

"That's not love, Lance."

"I don't need a biology lesson, Stephanie. This is love—heart, mind, body, and spirit. A love that says it wants you and only you, now and always. A lifetime commitment—the 'until death do us part' kind."

She shuddered. The euphoria of the previous moment receded, leaving reality with all its fears and apprehensions. "Lance, don't."

Releasing his hold on her, he demanded, "Why?"

"Because you are complicating things. You know me, you know our agreement," she hedged, closing her heart to him.

"Our agreement is a business arrangements, pure and simple—good for you and me. The way I feel about you is something entirely separate. I want to spend every moment with you—for the rest of my life and down through eternity if that is possible."

Why couldn't they remain friends—partners with a common goal, a comfortable relationship based on mutual respect? So much safer, the warm esteem of friendship than these searing emotions of love.

She pushed against him, fighting to be free—free from an emotion that might enslave her. "You don't know what you mean. It will completely destroy what we have."

"Stephanie, how can the way I feel about you destroy

you, destroy us?" His eyes, usually alert and confident, pleaded for an explanation he could understand. "I will never take advantage of you—I want the best for you, to take care of you—"

"I never want anyone to take care of me—don't you see? I never want to be dependent on anyone, not you, not *anyone*," she said, her teeth clenched, trying to bring her conflicting emotions under control.

Lance dropped his arms, his handsome features sharp as he fought his own battle with bewilderment and frustration. This was a Stephanie he'd never seen. "Why are you afraid of me, Steph? Is it because we've only known each other a few months? Have I done anything to cause you to distrust me?"

"This talk of marriage frightens me."

"Why, Stephanie?"

"I'm not sure you'd understand."

"Was it another man? Have you been hurt?" he gently probed, determination set in his face.

"No."

" What, then? What *are* you afraid of?"

"I. . .I don't like what love can do to a person," she answered uneasily as memories of her mother pierced her heart. She dropped her head, unable once again to meet the intensity in his gaze.

His dark brows lifted questioningly, but he remained silent, his eyes demanding an explanation. She turned away from those disturbing eyes. How could she make him understand that years before she'd determined not to love? She tried to calm her racing heart—to put substance to the old resolutions that ruled her—yet it was hard when he stood so near.

She walked away from him, putting more distance between them. His very nearness stirred a response in her that was stronger than her stubborn will. She must have time to sort out her answer, to make him know that they had no future together beyond a warm friendship and a business venture.

Her tortuous thoughts propelled her on. Finally she almost ran down the rocky pathway, stopping only when she reached the end of the path. There a rock wall separated it from a sheer cliff that fell straight to the rocks and pounding surf below. A stiff northeastern breeze blew, and she knew despite the cloudless sky that a late summer storm brewed somewhere out in that vast ocean. It blew her silken hair in wild profusion around her head, whipping her face, then lifting it to trail behind her, catching the light in silver ribbons. She caught her breath in a ragged shudder, half sob. *Why does he have to complicate things? Why can't he just accept things as they are?* Her eyes mirrored the sea's stormy turbulence. She clenched and unclenched a tiny, competent fist, frustration framed in every movement.

Suddenly a quiet, firm voice spoke in her ear and two strong hands gripped her shoulder. "Steph, you can't run far enough to get away from me."

Lance gently turned her to him. With her back to the ocean, her heart pounded her ears in cadence with the power and force of the water below. "Darling, tell me what you're afraid of. Let me help you," he pleaded as he searched her eyes for an answer.

Stephanie was powerless to answer. Her stubborn will weakened as her demanding heart threatened to betray her.

A half-smile brushed Lance's lips, but only fierce

determination lighted the eyes that held hers.

"I'm not afraid," she denied, "It's just that I'm not ready for this. . ."

"Ready for what—love? I love you, Stephanie. That's the simple truth. I'm not talking about any other relationship but that. I've never been in love before. I've been infatuated by beauty and charm, but never this. Honey, you turn the morning on for me!"

Stephanie, mesmerized by the raw emotion she saw in his eyes, reached up and pressed her fingers against his lips. She moaned softly, "No, don't. Don't, Lance. You mustn't talk that way—feel that way. I can't."

"You can't what? You feel the same way I do. I can tell—the way your eyes look at me when I come in a room, the soft smile that's mine alone. You can deny it with your lips, but that doesn't change your heart."

Stephanie opened her lips to speak but the denial died in her throat.

Lance rushed on in a torrent of words, releasing his pent up emotions. His eyes were midnight blue with intensity as he tried to convince her. "I'm not pressing you now— it's too early in our relationship for that. I just want to spend more time with you—time for our love to grow. It's only just beginning. It's fragile, but it's there. Give it time—give us time." His eyes were smiling, filled with a pleading, tender patience that melted Stephanie's heart.

"No pressure?"

"No, just time together—sharing our work, our hopes and dreams, the summer sunsets, the morning mists rolling in from the ocean." He beamed an encouraging smile. "Agreed?"

She narrowed her eyes, once again able to look him in

the face, a tenuous smile tugging at her mouth, "Time. I need time to sort things out. To search my heart. If you'll give me time."

"Are you ready to tell me what you meant about not loving anyone?"

"Not just yet, but someday."

"I'll wait until you're ready, and Steph, you're worth waiting for and so is our love."

Stephanie turned wide, troubled eyes to his. "I don't want to hurt you, Lance."

A broad grin parted his face. His eyes danced as with some mysterious knowledge that spelled victory. "You won't, my dear. You love me too much, whether or not you know it." Then putting his hands on each side of her face, he lifted it up, locking her eyes to his. "Stephanie, I'll never take advantage of you. I only want your happiness. Trust me. Follow your heart."

His eyes darkened once again with emotion before he bent his head and claimed Stephanie's lips in a long kiss.

Lance released her with a slight smile. The warmth of her response had answered his question. A soft mist in her shining eyes proclaimed a woman on the brink of love.

eight

By mid-afternoon, the storm, which had announced its coming in the gentle ocean breeze of the night before, hit full blast. It deposited its fury on the manicured lawns, and its gale force winds bowed the tall, stately trees as if they were young saplings. High water flooded the main road leading to the inn, and the small group of people housed there were like an island.

Stephanie paced up and down the parlor. Every few minutes, she glanced out the window and shuddered.

The lights flickered, and she prayed the power would stay on, but she breathed a silent thanks that Lance had insisted on putting in the auxiliary power unit. He was right again. Accommodating guests was a big responsibility.

Abigail walked through the room, pausing to speak to several people. Stephanie noticed her usual bright smile appeared forced. When she arrived at Stephanie's side, she turned to look out the window, worry written on her face.

"Have you seen Lance?" Abby questioned, her voice tense.

"No, I imagine he is stranded in his cottage. Told me he had a lot of paperwork to do."

"I helped him, so he finished about mid-morning. *Carefree's* crew had asked him to check on a little problem they were having with the sloop so he left for the boathouse," Abigail explained.

"He what?" Stephanie's voice rose in alarm.

"That's not the worst of it," Abigail exclaimed, her eyes bright with anxiety. "He said he thought he'd take *Carefree* out. You know how much he'd wanted to."

Fear and regret descended on Stephanie, almost suffocating her. She remembered. How many bright and shining days of summer had she put Lance off when he'd asked her to go? She had been too busy working, trying to prove to him her worth, her independence, and now. . .

She rejected the thought. He mustn't be lost. She could call the rescue unit. But how? The telephones were out and only the boathouse housed the ship-to-shore and short-wave radios.

Abigail tugged at her arm. "Stephanie, did you hear me? I said Lance may be on *Carefree*. What can we do?"

Darkness settled around Stephanie's eyes, and she turned back toward the voice of her friend. The only thing she could see was Abigail's face, her worried eyes. "Didn't he know. . .about. . .the storm?" The words stumbled out haltingly.

"No. Just laughed when I warned him. Said I was talking to a sailor who'd been in some real storms before. You know how he is."

Out of Stephanie's anguish, a bitter smile tugged at her mouth and she answered softly, "Oh, yes. I know how he is."

Maybe, maybe he was still in his cottage. She strained to see it. No lights. No Lance. No happiness, only pain. She turned from the window.

"Abigail, I'm going to borrow Randy's Jeep and go to the boathouse."

"You can't—" Abigail started to protest.

"I have to."

Stephanie refused to allow anyone to go with her. Knowing the risks involved did not prepare her for the perilous journey. Trees blocked the lane, and the Jeep slid as she left the road to drive around them. Without four-wheel drive, the trip would have been impossible. At times, the wind almost set the small vehicle off its wheels. Stephanie strained to see through gray sheets of rain.

Finally, the lane began its gentle descent to the inlet and boathouse. Water cascaded down the ramp with such force that Stephanie feared the vehicle would be swept into the inlet. Finally reaching the safety of the buildings, she peered anxiously toward the small sound. Her long white sloop with the bright blue stripes was not in its slip. Hope for Lance disintegrated in one long shuddering sob.

Cold rain mingled with warm tears streamed unnoticed down her face, leaving a salty taste on her lips. As she ran toward the building and her one beacon of hope, she uttered a pathetic prayer of confession, "Oh, God, protect him. I do need him. I've fought it so hard—bring him back to me."

All through the night, Stephanie kept watch by the radio. It crackled and popped and occasionally voices spoke, but no message came for her.

The inlet offered some protection from the wind, and she was thankful for the sturdy comfort of the building. It resembled a clubhouse with its fireplace and kitchen area.

She built a fire and put on a pot of coffee—for her and for Lance. He'd need it when he came back. She surveyed the well-stocked cooler for food. Satisfied, she noted that it had eggs. He'd be hungry as a bear.

A smile softened the lines of worry and fatigue that bound her face. His hearty appetite amazed her, yet his body remained lean and trim. Abigail said he ran every day—she hadn't known that. Her heart constricted and she felt a pang of jealousy toward her friend. How many other things about him did she take for granted? The wan smile faded, and she put her head in her hands.

Had she been so involved with their project, with proving her worth, her independence, that she'd failed in a more important issue? Like the brilliance of a lighting bolt, the answer came. If she'd failed, it had been because of fear—fear to let herself love. That fear had set her priorities and driven her to prove her independence, to deny her need for anyone.

Stephanie's eyes filled with tears that slowly made a warm, wet pathway down her cheeks. She wept bitter tears of regret—the regret of wasted moments. Now, too late, she knew her feeling for Lance superseded the fear that held her in bondage. He had wanted to help her, to show her that love didn't always enslave, but she'd refused and now she might never know the joy of love as God had intended it. Oh, yes. Her fear had been wrong, so wrong. If God would only give her another chance.

With shuddering sobs, she emptied her heart to God, pouring out her fear and confusion. Slowly, Stephanie's sobs subsided, and a quiet assurance calmed her. God would give her another chance.

The hours dragged on, but she refused to doubt. Come morning, Lance would return.

A gray dawn proclaimed morning. Stephanie had dropped off to sleep from sheer weariness, but a strangely familiar sound jerked her awake. The wind and rain had ceased their howling. She ran to the door facing the water and saw a mist rolling in from the sea.

The light of a coast guard cutter sliced through the mist and raked the shore. The boat continued its unswerving course straight toward her dock.

With her heart in her throat, Stephanie opened the door and stepped through just as the boat pulled up and a tall, bedraggled figure dressed in jeans and a plaid shirt stepped onto the slick boards of the landing.

Lance bent his head to look back into the boat and, with a nonchalant salute, bid the crew goodbye. His wet clothes were plastered to him, and his hair was flat and dark with water. A day-old beard darkened his face, and he walked with a slight limp.

A cry of sheer joy wrenched from Stephanie's throat as she ran down the slippery dock. Giving no heed to her safety or his, she hurled herself into his arms, sobbing.

With an impudent grin, he lifted her head and lightly kissed her cheek. "What's the matter, Steph? You lose something?"

The emotions of fear and worry that she had battled all night exploded in angry relief. "Lancelot Donovan, where have you been? Don't you tease me about this. I thought . . .I thought. . ." A heart-wrenching sob escaped and she could go no further.

"You thought what, my darling?"

"I. . .I thought. . .I'd lost you," the independent Stephanie Haynes confessed between sobs.

The impudent light left Lance's eyes. Holding her like a small child, he brushed the damp blond curls from her face and crooned softly, "Never. Nothing can take me away from you."

She looked up, her eyes shining with soft radiance, and whispered, "I know." Then dropping her head on his shoulder, she nestled in the warm security of his embrace.

While Lance changed into some dry clothes he had left in his locker, Stephanie cooked a quick breakfast. As they ate, he told her about his afternoon adventures.

He'd sailed out of the inlet into the sea for about an hour when he'd discovered a problem with the rudder. Nearing Evergreen Island, he'd decided to dock on the leeward side and fix it. Finding a protected inlet, he anchored and lowered the sails.

He failed to notice the approaching storm until he finished the repairs. "Even for a daredevil like me, that storm was too rough, so I hoisted the storm sail to keep her pointed into the wind. Then I dropped both anchors, making sure they were on the bottom securely about fifty yards offshore so she wouldn't blow aground. I had one cold swim back to shore." Involuntarily, he shuddered.

Lance continued, "When I reached the island, I headed for higher ground. My ship-to-shore radio wouldn't work, but I did have emergency flares, so I climbed the one high bluff on Evergreen and found a small cave to ward off the elements. I weathered the storm there until the coast guard came and picked me up. They said they saw my flare because you had radioed them. They were a welcome sight. The cave kept the trees from falling on me, but the water blew in. I thought I'd never be warm again—that is until I stepped on the dock."

Stephanie blushed and dropped her head, suddenly shy with him. "What. . .what about *Carefree*?"

"I think she survived it okay. I didn't have time to

examine her before I left. They are going to carry me back over there to pick her up this afternoon. Do you think you could find time to help me bring her back?" Although thoughts of her responsibilities bombarded Stephanie's mind, she nodded her head without a moment's hesitation. Her priorities had changed. God had given her that chance. The chance to know Lance better, to test their love.

As it does so often after a storm, the sun shone that day with an added radiance, and the sky hung a cloudless blue. Lance arrived at the lodge shortly after three with a picnic hamper. He looked as if he'd not missed a minute of sleep.

His eyes brightened at the sight of Stephanie. With her blond hair pulled back in a pony tail and denim shorts and red shirt, she looked like a teenager. Had anyone cared to ask her, she could have told them she felt like one. Something strange had happened to her during the tortuous hours before dawn. She was able to walk across the storm-wrecked lawn without a backward glance at the work waiting to be done. Somehow it would get done, but for right now, her only thought was the man beside her and the adventure of being together that awaited them.

A radiant smile greeted Lance, and Abigail, noting it, said mischievously, "You sure you don't want me to go so you can stay here and direct the clean-up crew?"

"Absolutely sure, Abby. I put this off for a whole summer. Lance and I are going for a sail." Slipping her hand in Lance's outstretched one, Stephanie added with eyes large and dark, "I almost waited too long."

The cutter met them at the dock, and a half hour later they were pulling into the calm inlet where *Carefree* bobbed up and down in the gentle swells.

Pulling up beside the sloop, the cutter soon had maneuvered in position to enable Lance and Stephanie to climb aboard her. After thoroughly checking the boat for damages, the couple smiled in agreement. The storm had taken no toll on their lovely boat. They would not be spending precious hours making repairs.

Lance looked at Stephanie mischievously. "Too bad you don't have your swim suit. I'd race you to the shore."

Stephanie laughed up at him, her eyes dancing. "You don't get off that easily, Sir Lancelot. I have my suit on, and I challenge you." She stepped from her shorts and removed her shirt, revealing a brightly colored maillot. Diving overboard, she swam swiftly through the cold water.

Before she reached shallow water, her teeth were chattering, and she shuddered at the thought of Lance's swim in the storm. Just then he swam up beside her. His powerful brown arms propelled him through the water, barely rippling the surface. Stephanie paused to marvel at Lance's strength and expertise. When he pulled half a length ahead of her, he turned on his back and splashed water in her face. "I win. Admit it. What's the prize?"

"I admit it—and the prize is you get to spend the afternoon with me, you lucky man."

"The most delightful prize I could imagine, my dear," he replied as they reached shallow water and ran splashing to shore.

The afternoon passed too quickly. They laughed, explored the island, and raced along the beach. Stephanie learned about Lance's family, his boyhood, and the things he liked to do. She discovered they shared many interests.

She reveled in the warm sense of contentment that she

felt in these shared moments with Lance. Other than hold her hand, he didn't touch her, but the warmth of his gaze was as tender as an embrace, setting her heart aglow.

Was this love? This total joy in being in the presence of the beloved. Not touching, yet united in spirit? This feeling of completeness? Was this why it could enslave?

For the first time since she had lost her parents, Stephanie understood her mother's tragic grief. Her eyes clouded.

Lance noticed. "What's the matter, Steph?"

She shook her head in half denial.

"You can't fool me. You've left me again. That mysterious something that keeps taking you away from me like some gate to your past slams shut, and you close me out. I don't like that. Don't you think it's time you told me?"

"Yes, but it's getting late, and I think we'd better get back to the boat. Besides aren't you hungry yet?"

"Sure. Love makes you that way. Aren't you hungry?" he countered.

"Come to think of it, I am. I believe I could eat a bear."

"There, that proves my point! See what love did for your appetite?" he insisted.

"You really think I'm in love, Lance?"

"No think to it. I know it. This one thing I know: We were meant for each other."

She remained quiet for a long moment, looking down at the sand. Her heart raced, but her lips refused to respond.

Lance placed his hand under her chin and lifted her head, forcing her eyes to meet his. Emotions struggled in the clear blue depths of hers. Then, hesitantly, she asked, "What do you mean by that?"

"I mean, pardner, we'll need to be finding a preacher man and get married up," he drawled in a perfect cowboy mimic.

Stephanie's brow creased, and she pulled her chin from his hand. "I don't think that something to tease about."

Lance looked at her long and hard. "I'm not teasing. I plan to marry you. I meant it when I told you that last spring, and I mean it now. The only thing I don't know is when. Two problems to that: your agreement and the success of these business ventures."

Stephanie shot him a puzzled look.

"Most of my worldly goods that I could 'thee endow' are tied up, and my success is riding on this film," Lance explained.

"You mean you couldn't afford to do these improvements on Boulder Bay?"

"Not if I didn't know it would pay off. Leasing it to the film company will get us the majority of our initial investment, and the free advertising the film will give us insures a successful season next year. No, my dear. It isn't the inn that's the problem; it's the film. In order to get the film rights I had to act quickly, and I invested far beyond what I usually do. I didn't have time to get a substantial number of investors, but I believed so strongly in the film's potential that I took the risk. Big investment means big return—or big loss."

"You mean you're the only investor?"

"No, I don't have that much capital or credit. Alana DeLue is the other major investor, and then we have a cartel of small investors."

"I thought she was the star."

"Yeh, that's part of the deal and great for me. Her name means box office clout, and that's the way she wanted it. Every producer in Hollywood wanted this story. It was a bidding situation, and when I got the opportunity, I had to move swiftly."

"You *outbid* everybody else?"

He looked sheepish. "Not exactly."

"Well?" she persisted.

"Strange set of circumstances. Guess you might say it was my unbeatable charm." He grinned disarmingly.

"Charm must be worth a lot in Hollywood."

"It is, but to tell you the truth, I think it must have been being at the right place at the right time."

"You mean divine appointment?"

"I'd say coincidence."

" I don't believe in coincidences, Lance."

"Yeh, I remember. You thought I was an answer to prayer." He smiled, but a hint of uncertainty touched his usual confident gaze.

"You were—and are."

"For whatever the reason, I got the script. I'm glad for the opportunity, but its success is not assured. I believe in the project, but even if production is finished on time and within the budget, it awaits a fickle public's response. No, until the cash registers start jingling substantially, I couldn't think of offering myself to you. Too much risk involved."

"Risk?"

"Yes, that I couldn't look after you the way I want to. Lady, I want to put the world at your feet debt free." His eyes crinkled with a merry grin, but Stephanie could see beyond the mirth. His eyes were serious.

Stephanie bit the corner of her lip, revealing the tips of her even white teeth, and remarked hesitantly, "I sincerely pray that it's going to be a success for your sake, but not for me, Lance. You mustn't do it for me. I don't want you or anyone to lay the world at my feet. In fact, I never intended to fall in love."

Stephanie whirled from Lance and ran into the surf, diving in just beyond the breakers. She swam fiercely, fleeing her unstable emotions. What had destroyed the peace and contentment of the afternoon? Why had fear reared its ugly head once more? And fear about what?

nine

Stephanie arrived at the boat before Lance and went below to towel off and change her clothes. She pulled her hair back in damp ringlets and touched her lips lightly with color.

The sun rested low over the horizon, and she pulled her jacket closer to her as she stepped out onto the deck. The evening breeze had a chill in it, and she was thankful she had brought the additional jeans and jacket.

Lance had *Carefree* underway by then. She went to sit beside him at the wheel. He'd exchanged his suit for white denim pants and a bright blue shirt that turned his eyes to cobalt. The power of his masculine good looks played havoc with her studied composure.

She took a deep breath and looked up at him. He ignored her presence, devoting his attention to the job at hand. Stephanie watched, entranced, then shifted uncomfortably. Seconds turned into minutes, and only the wind snapping the sails broke the silence. Stephanie understood. Lance was determined that she would take the initiative. Stubbornly she kept silent. Didn't he care? What had happened to the warm rapport of this afternoon?

She flinched. She had destroyed it by running away. Now it was up to her, not Lance, to restore that intimacy.

They had crossed the open water between the small island and the mainland. The dock and boathouse loomed ahead. Stubbornly, Stephanie remained silent, the words she needed to speak locked in her mind and heart.

Finally Lance maneuvered *Carefree* into her slip. Without speaking, Stephanie threw herself into assisting him by dropping the sails and securing the boat.

When they had finished, Lance nodded toward the picnic basket and asked tersely, "Would you like to eat here or at the boathouse?"

"The boathouse, but...." Stephanie walked up to Lance and stood in front of him. She placed one small hand on his chest and toyed with one of his buttons, refusing to look up.

"Yes?" he asked.

"I'm sorry if I ruined our afternoon."

"I am, too, Stephanie. I love you and you love me, but our future relationship depends on you. I don't understand your fear, and until you deal with it or at least trust me enough to let me help you with it, we're at a stalemate."

"I have—did deal with it—last night."

"That doesn't explain what happened today."

She smiled slightly and raised her head to look directly at him. "Old responses are hard to break. I didn't want to talk about it, but I owe you an explanation. It was what you said—about laying the world at my feet, taking care of me. In a way it sounds like enslavement."

"Enslavement?" His eyebrows came together, astonishment sharpening his countenance.

"My idea of marriage is partnership," Stephanie continued.

Lance shook his head, puzzled.

"It was my parents," Stephanie explained. "What you said reminded me of their relationship. You can't imagine what that did to my mother."

"Not unless you tell me," he encouraged gently, his eyes

softening.

"My mother was so dependent on my father that when he died, she couldn't go on living. He was her world, her only world—almost her god."

"Darling, that wasn't a normal or healthy love."

"I know. I felt disgust for what I thought was my mother's weakness—until I met you. Lance, the way I feel when I'm with you is overpowering. It frightens me because—how do I know that I won't react like she did? After all, she's my mother."

"Did she have a strong faith?"

"I don't know. She never discussed it with me. She was religious, but somehow it didn't influence her life."

"There you're altogether different. Who taught you about faith?"

"My father. He had a strong faith in Jesus Christ. He had accepted Christ as his Savior, but beyond that, my dad trusted Jesus as the Lord of his life."

"You mean he was a strong man who had confidence in himself and could handle problems?"

"Not exactly. Lance, do you ever have a moment of self-doubt?"

"Nope. I know what it takes to get a job done, and I'm willing to pay the price. I haven't had a problem yet I couldn't solve, and I'm confident now. I just don't quite know what the timing will be."

"Doesn't God-given talent have anything to do with it?"

"Uh, maybe, but I'm inclined to think God leaves it up to us to make a success of it, don't you?"

"Well, yes. I think He wants us to be diligent and work at what He gives us to do, but it's more than that. He has a purpose for us—a special place for us to fill. That's why

He gives us talent. Don't you think so?"

"No, not really. I think God is too busy to be concerned about whether or not I produce a certain movie. I think He gives us the talent, and it's up to us to get out and find the opportunities."

"Then why are you filming this particular story?"

"Just like I said. I think it's outstanding enough to be a blockbuster. That means money, prestige, and success—not to mention being in a position to offer myself to you."

Stephanie couldn't suppress a smile at his candor. "The story is uplifting. It will leave the world a better place. Don't you think that God might have a reason for wanting it produced?"

"I dunno. Never thought about it before."

"Why have you produced the films that you have?"

"Because I believe that wholesome entertainment is a better investment. It'll bring in more dollars."

"Lance!"

"Okay. I don't want my name on anything that would violate my moral principles, but I don't think God has time to read scripts. It'd be hard for me to believe that He's interested in the movies I produce. Seems to me He's got more important matters to contend with than my day-to-day affairs."

"I guess you've never learned just how important a person is to God, Lance."

"Nope, I guess I haven't. Where did you get that notion?" he asked lightly, but his eyes probed yearningly.

"When I had nowhere else to turn. That's where most people learn, Lance—out of desperation—and that's a pity. We could save ourselves so much anxiety and pain if we were willing to discover God's love and concern earlier."

"Perhaps you're right, Stephanie. I've just never encountered anything I couldn't handle. I've never questioned it. Now I understand that God had to have a plan for salvation. I accepted Jesus Christ when I was a child. I knew that He had paid the price for my sin on the cross and I needed to ask forgiveness for that and invite Him into my life."

"Well, where's He been since?"

Lance chuckled humorlessly. "I've acknowledged my responsibility to Him for moral decisions, but the rest of my life. . . . I sort of thought He just equipped me in the beginning and the rest was up to me—you know, direction, sink or swim, all those issues."

Stephanie smiled at him sadly. "I hope you discover the truth before you get in a desperate situation. God is interested in every area of our lives. His interest gives us purpose, an excitement in everything that we do—an added dimension as it were."

"Is that what's different about you? The secret that gives you that special glow?"

"I didn't know I had one." She wrinkled her nose at him, her blue eyes wide and questioning.

"Most of the time. Sometimes it gets clouded over—like a few moments ago. For someone so strong in her faith, you seem to have short-circuited it where love is concerned. How can fear and faith live together?"

The truth of his question probed Stephanie's soul, and she paused before answering. Tears filled her eyes as she explained haltingly, "I struggled with that question all last night when I thought you might be gone. I asked God for another chance, and He gave it to me."

"What are you going to do with it?"

"Not run away from it again. That was just an emotional reaction earlier this afternoon. I know now that I can learn not to fear love—and you're right. The love Mom had for Dad was not the way God planned love to be. But I think I must blame Dad some, too."

"Why?"

"Because he let my mother depend on him. He never prepared her for eventualities."

"He took good care of her."

"Too good. That's what I'm talking about. Our ideas of love and faith, too, are so different. Even when I put aside my fears, I don't know how we can reconcile our differences."

"Don't you think my faith can grow?"

"Are you willing for it to?"

"I don't know if I can ever see life as simply as you" came his honest answer.

"You mean you want to be in charge of your life and mine?"

"I want to take care of you."

"You want to take care of me, but I want a partnership—a relationship where I can contribute, do my part."

"What if I do want to take care of you? I don't see that your father did anything wrong. That's a man's pride, taking care of his woman."

"To the point she can't survive without him?"

"Sounds romantic."

"I'm not talking about a Hollywood script. I'm talking about a tragedy that I don't want to repeat. If you can't understand what I'm talking about, then perhaps we don't have a foundation for a lasting relationship. Lance, I will have to be able to share my faith with the man I marry, and he'll have to need me as much as I need him. He must be someone who'll let me share his heartaches and defeats as well as his victories. I never want to be on a pedestal to be adored and worshiped. I want a man who's strong enough to let me help him."

"You want a weak man, Stephanie?"

"No, a strong man who needs me."

"I need you."

"How?"

"I need your love."

"That's not enough."

"Stephanie, I don't want you to support me. I want to look after you. I have a need to take care of you."

"What if something happens and you can't? Will you stop loving me? Will I stop loving you?"

"Nothing is going to happen. I'll see to that!"

"That's just my point. Will our relationship be based on your ability to take care of me? If you take care of me well, then I'm to love you lots, and if you take care of me less, I love you less? Do you see what you're reducing love to?"

"Is it so wrong for a man to want to provide for the woman he loves?"

She smiled, shrugging sadly. "No, Lance. That's a God-given instinct within a man—to be the protector and the provider. But with some men, it has evolved into a macho self-image that's destructive. Failures are bound to happen. They come to every life. I don't think you would let me share them with you. Lance, the real mark of a strong man is one who can admit he needs help—from God and from his wife."

Pain sharpened Lance's handsome features, and his

thick dark brows knit together. Stephanie saw uncertainty and something akin to anger flare in them briefly before he answered tersely, "Maybe you're right. Perhaps I'm not the man for you because with every fiber of me, body and soul, I want to love, protect, and take care of you. If that weakens me in your eyes, then I'm weak." He turned abruptly and walked away toward the road home, his hunger and the filled hamper forgotten.

Tears of frustration streamed down Stephanie's cheeks as a sob caught in her throat. She wanted to run after him, but instead she watched him walk away. All her resolutions had dissolved. She knew the heart-wrenching truth— weak or strong, success or failure, she loved Lance and always would. Enslaved or free he was the only man she could ever love. But did she dare?

Stephanie did not know how long she sat huddled on the dock after Lance left, but unnoticed, night had descended.

Car lights bounced off the wide drive and curved downward as a vehicle started its descent to the landing. Stephanie ran her hand through her tousled curls, muttering, "I must look a sight." She did. With eyes red from weeping and rumpled clothing, she squared her small shoulders and stood up, dreading to face anyone, except Lance. Maybe, just maybe, he'd returned.

Abigail's bright little car dispelled that hope.

"Stephanie, you down there? I can't see. Why don't you turn on the dock lights?" Abby called as she alighted from the car. As soon as her eyes became accustomed to the darkness, she spotted Stephanie.

"Oh, thank goodness! Martha needed you so I came for—you look a mess!" she exclaimed as Stephanie stepped into the harsh circle of car light.

Stephanie retorted with a bitter smile, "If you ever need a lift, call for Abigail."

"Oh shucks, Stephanie, don't complain. You're the only woman I know who can still look beautiful when she's a mess. What happened? You and Lance, wasn't it? I knew it. I saw him come storming home without you."

Stephanie smiled ruefully at her friend's nonstop conversation.

Abigail saw the smile. "That's better. I knew it couldn't be the end of the world. Just a lover's quarrel. Happens all the time."

Much to Stephanie's chagrin, the tears she thought she had exhausted began again. "It's more than that—much more."

"Well, Steph, it can't be as bad as that. You two are the greatest people I've ever known. You seem made for each other."

"Don't sa...say that, Abby. That's what he said," Stephanie sobbed.

"Seems to me he's right. Want to tell me about it?" Abigail gently probed as she started the car and expertly maneuvered it up the gentle grade.

Stephanie gave Abby an abbreviated account of what had occurred.

Her friend remained silent until Stephanie had finished and then observed, "I can understand where you're coming from, Stephanie, but the problems don't seem insurmountable."

"I think Lance thought so."

"Oh, he was just mad. You had injured his male ego, and he's stubborn, too. One of the reasons he's been so successful is his stubborn will."

"That's what worries me, Abby. He has such a strong will, how can his faith grow when he doesn't even think he needs any?"

"Well, it's harder for men to let go and step out on faith. It's a male characteristic. They like to be in control. But from my experience, God has His own way about putting us in situations that we can't handle any other way. And as for you—you're pretty independent, too, young lady. Do you have any idea how many girls would give their right arms and twenty years of their lives to have a man like Lance Donovan want to take care of them like he wants to take care of you?"

"I know. The way I feel doesn't make sense. But, Abby, I feel so overpowered when Lance is near. I find myself forgetting everything but him. I can't let that happen. Marriage is forever, and I believe there are certain ingredients that are basic for its survival—a shared faith and a shared concept of life. Other differences can be worked out by compromise, but not those."

"I admire your stamina, Stephanie. It's not the first time I've seen you risk everything for your convictions. If there's anything I can do to help, just let me know. I think the world of you both."

"Both?" Stephanie looked squarely at her friend, a question, not voiced, in her eyes.

Abigail flushed and answered firmly, "Yes, both. Stephanie, I'd be deaf, dumb, and blind if I hadn't noticed how handsome Lance is, but believe me, he's not my type. Even if he were, his eyes see only you. You've got nothing to worry about there, anyway. Now you go wash and get all dolled up. Dinner is served in an hour. It's a special bash tonight—all Boulder Bay people—and Martha prepared a treat."

Stephanie took a long leisurely soak in the oversized tub with claw feet. After placing witch hazel pads over her eyes to reduce the swelling, she deftly applied a little makeup to cover the emotional ravages of the afternoon. She piled her hair high on her head in a cascade of curls and put on a long black evening gown that molded her slender body and emphasized her blond beauty. She put on her mother's tear-drop diamond earrings and dabbed perfume behind her ears.

Glancing in the mirror, she gave herself a wry smile. "Head held high, Stephanie, and no one will guess the pain searing your insides. Not even Lance."

Tears welled in her eyes, and she whispered his name softly, caressing the sound of it with her lips.

Soft music played as she descended the stairs, and voices raised in animated conversation. People stood in groups drinking hot cider and eating hors d'oeuvres. Abby had been right. Tonight was special. Looking around her, Stephanie frowned. There were some faces she didn't recognize and one face she looked for and didn't find.

Stephanie reached out and took the crystal cup that John handed her. She smiled up at him—he, too, looked handsome and distinguished in his dark suit. There was Martha in her best gray taffeta. A celebration of sorts, but for what?

A bell tinkled, and Abigail, dressed in a short, pale yellow gown, stood on the stairway. "Friends, I would like to propose a toast to Martha and John. It's their fiftieth wedding anniversary."

She turned her head toward them and raised her cup

high. "May your second fifty be as lovely as your first. By the way, how old were you when you got married? You're much too young to have been married that long."

"I married her when she's a girl of sixteen and I's a lad of seventeen, but it's been my love what's kept her young," John spoke up with uncharacteristic boldness. Then he planted a kiss firmly on the mouth of his blushing bride, and the crowd roared with good-natured laughter and cheers of "Hear, Hear!!"

A lump knotted in Stephanie's throat at the mist of love softly shining in Martha's eyes. What would it be like to share a love like theirs for half a century and longer? What would it be like to share a love with Lance for. . . . She didn't finish the thought, for she heard familiar deep tones behind her as he entered the room and she turned to meet him, a warm greeting on her lips and soft shining eyes.

It died without utterance, for she turned to meet a pair of fiery ebony eyes in a small face with perfectly chiseled features. Abundant dark hair set off the woman's exotic beauty, and her red gown clung sensuously to every curve, dipping low at the bodice. Diamond bracelets graced her arms as did diamond rings her hands. Around her slender ivory neck hung one exquisite diamond, large and brilliant.

The beauty paused, one arm entwined in Lance's, as the dark eyes raked Stephanie from head to toe. A malicious smile played at one corner of her mouth, and she remarked in perfectly modulated tones for all to hear, "So this is the little country girl you're going to turn into a princess, Lance, darling."

Stephanie bit back an angry retort, but before she could answer, Lance winked at her, responding smoothly, "She's already a princess. Stephanie Haynes, may I present Alana DeLue. Her bark is much worse than her bite."

Alana gave Lance a throaty laugh. "Lance, you will completely destroy my image."

He bent his dark golden head to hers attentively and replied, "Not a chance, my dear. Your beauty and grace speak for you."

"Now that's the Donovan charm to which I'm accustomed," she smiled up at him. Turning to Stephanie, Alana held out her hand. "Miss Haynes, glad to have you on board. I'm looking forward to working with you. It seems that our Lance here is fairly moonstruck with you. Now I can see why."

Stephanie stared in disbelieving wonder. As quickly as a stage curtain can be drawn, the facade disappeared from Alana DeLue. The fiery eyes now contained genuine warmth and friendliness, but tinged with something else—pain, longing. Stephanie couldn't decide. Alana's beauty was genuine, and if Stephanie were any judge, it had been forged in pain.

Lance had known Alana for years. Their affection for each other was obvious to the most casual observer. Stephanie's observance was anything but. How had he resisted her, or had he?

Looking into the eyes of the beautiful woman, Stephanie experienced a new kind of fear. Cold, icy fingers gripped her heart as she responded stiffly, "I don't know what Lance has told you, but we're *all* excited about having you and the rest of the crew here. I didn't expect you until next week. I'm afraid you have caught us in the aftermath of a storm."

Alana raised a hand as if to brush such concerns aside.

"Lance told me all about it. The place is lovely, and Lance's cottage will be just perfect for me."

Stephanie's face blanched, and she turned questioning eyes toward Lance.

"Guess I fixed it up too well. I hope you don't mind a cluttered office, Alana, because that's a working apartment, and I'm not moving that office even for you, my lovely," he warned, tweaking her chin with his finger.

"No bother. Having you around again will be wonderful. It's been a long time, darling," she answered softly.

"Too long," he agreed.

Stephanie stirred uncomfortably. Unable to respond, she was grateful when Abby's voice broke in. "Miss DeLue, I'm Abigail Burnes, Lance's secretary. If you need anything, just call and I'll get it. I'm sorry your cottage was damaged by the storm."

Alana smiled at Abigail, giving her the same appraising look she had given Stephanie. "Thank you, Abigail, but I'll be fine. I've taken possession of Lance's cottage."

Abigail's lips smiled, but her eyes flew to Stephanie in alarm. "Uh—"

Stephanie found her voice and smoothly replied, "That's quite all right, Abby. If it suits Lance, how can we object? Right, Lance?"

Alana turned her dark eyes on Stephanie, wide and knowing. They sparkled with amusement. Stephanie flushed, realizing the beautiful star had read her heart.

Lance, oblivious to the undercurrent going on responded, "Right. Now where's dinner? Seems I missed mine somehow, and suddenly I'm hungry."

Lance's remark pierced Stephanie's heart as the painful memories of their afternoon together blinded her. She turned from the striking couple before they could see the pain in her eyes and mumbled, "I think dinner will be served momentarily."

"Alana, I can't wait for you to try the food here. But mind, you'll have to be very careful. I won't have a chubby leading lady," Lance chortled as they moved across the room and away from Stephanie without a backward glance.

Abby looked at Stephanie and raised her eyebrows. In a low voice, she remarked, "Wow! She'll certainly liven things up around here."

"Well, she's the star," Stephanie responded with a sad shrug. Squaring her shoulders, she lifted her head and moved across the room with the art and grace of a seasoned performer.

That night Stephanie gave the first performance of her life, and it dazzled. While inside she mourned with the regrets of what might have been, outside she sparkled with wit and beauty. Periodically, she looked up to catch Lance's questioning eyes on her. This was a Stephanie he'd never seen—a chic and sophisticated beauty whose charm had completely captivated the cosmopolitan group. Had he just witnessed the metamorphosis of a country girl?

ten

Lance would never know what Stephanie's performance cost her or the agony of uncertainty that she carried to bed with her that night.

The memory of Lance walking away from her in anger and the image of his head bent to the flashing-eyed beauty in his cottage seared her mind and denied her the oblivion of a dreamless sleep. Even in slumber, she wept.

Despite a fitful rest, her weary body demanded restoration after two nights without sleep, and Stephanie stirred only when Abigail pounded at her door.

"Sorry you missed the hot breakfast, Steph. This was the best I could do. Kitchen is all cranked up for lunch." Abby explained cheerfully, a breakfast tray in her arms.

Stephanie smiled weakly and ran her hand through her tousled hair. "Why didn't you wake me?"

"Because you haven't had any sleep in two nights."

"How do you know that?"

"Because I'm a woman, and I've been in love."

Stephanie raised an inquisitive brow as she took a sip of coffee, "You were in love?"

Abby shrugged nonchalantly while pain shadowed her eyes. "Yeah, loved and lost."

"I'm sorry, Abby. I didn't know."

"It was for the best—totally incompatible. But painful all the same. It still hurts sometimes. I'm sure, despite the pain, that I made the right decision. Anyway, he's married

121

now."

"I guess that's some consolation—that you made the right decision. Do you think I did?"

"Only you can determine that, Stephanie. Certain things are essential for a happy marriage—a shared faith is one of them. But if Lance tries to have a faith like yours just to please you, that won't work either."

"Oh, I know, Abby! But the issue is too vital to ignore. I guess I've lost him."

"Stephanie Haynes, you have forgotten something. God is in the life-changing business, not you. It's not too late for that, you know."

"Maybe not, but won't it be hard for even God to work in Lance's life with that beautiful Alana DeLue on his arm, not to mention in his apartment—maybe his bed?"

Abby burst into laughter at the woe be gone look on her friend's face. "Boy, are you borrowing trouble. You know Lance! Now trust him."

"Well, he's a man, and how could any man resist a temptation like that?"

"He loves *you!*"

"Does he? You weren't there when he walked away."

"No, but I know Lance. He's aggressive and used to getting what he wants. Your conditions angered and frustrated him. He'll be back. He loves you too much."

"But it wouldn't do any good, Abby. I don't want him to change just to please me. He'd end up resenting me. There just isn't any solution."

"The game's not over yet. Now you pull yourself together and get dressed. We've got two days' work to do in three hours. I could strangle Miss Hollywood for showing up with her entourage a week early!"

Stephanie laughed despite herself. "Did she say why she arrived early?"

Abby shrugged her shoulders. "She didn't talk it over with me. Are you going to get dressed, or are you coming down in that robe? I mean it. We've got to hurry!"

"Okay. It won't take me any time to shower and change."

"That's more like it. Work hard—it helps. I found that out," Abby responded as she closed the door behind her.

Abby's assessment proved correct. The early arrival of the rest of the crew pushed the Boulder Bay staff almost beyond endurance. The sets were readied and production started a week ahead of schedule, pleasing Lance. He rushed from set to set and barked commands to the crews. Alana DeLue stuck to him like his shadow.

Stephanie managed to miss Lance at meals. She ate early or late and stayed as busy as did he. She and Abby managed the Herculean task of repairs and cleanup after the storm.

One evening while Stephanie pored over the additional invoices, Abby slipped quietly into her office. As Stephanie ran a tape totaling up the final expenses, Abby peered over her shoulder and gave a low whistle. "That storm was expensive."

"Yes, it looks like I'm going to have to ask Lance for more money instead of giving some back to him. I hate that—for more reasons than one. At least I'd hoped to prove acceptable as a business partner."

"Stephanie, you couldn't help the storm."

"All the same...."

"All the same, I have good news for you. The insurance

company called earlier today and said that we had full coverage after all. I went in to town this afternoon and picked up the check. Here you are, boss lady. Now let me see you smile."

"Abby, how did you manage that?" Stephanie gasped.

"I've been negotiating with them for days. Finally, I called the insurance commissioner, and we got our check."

"What would I ever do without you, Abby?"

"My aim is to be indispensable. By the way, you need to be thinking about adding to our staff. Before the summer's out, you and I won't be able to handle this business efficiently."

"Who do you think we need?"

"A comptroller and legal help, but I don't know where to find them since Emerald Cove is short on professional people—at least when it comes to finding someone who isn't already buttonholed by Jay Dalton or Howard Jarrett." Abby shuddered involuntarily.

"You still think they haven't given up on us?"

"I know they haven't."

"Well, we haven't had any problems so far."

"Restorations weren't complete until now. I think Dalton's been biding his time. By the way, I'm almost positive that he passed me on the road to town when I was coming back."

"Could be. Some of the workmen said he'd been observing our progress."

"But that's not all. It looked like Alana DeLue was in the car with him."

"You must be mistaken, Abby. How could she know Jay Dalton?" Stephanie questioned.

"I don't know. You tell me."

Stephanie held the insurance check in her hands for a long time after Abby left, staring at it unseeingly as she considered what her friend had said. Hiring more personnel was something she'd have to discuss with Lance. Her hands grew cold. They had not talked since the day at the dock; she'd deliberately avoided him. But even if she hadn't, it would be difficult to deliberate business concerns with Alana DeLue glued to his side.

Stephanie grimaced in distaste, then laughed aloud. "I'm acting like a high school sophomore who's been jilted. Despite our personal problems, Lance and I are very compatible business partners. I think I'll walk over there tonight and talk to him or at least make an appointment for tomorrow."

She slipped quietly from her office and walked slowly across the lawn toward the bluff and the cottages. Reaching Lance's cottage, her sneakers propelled her silently across the wide brick porch. Just as she raised her hand to knock, she saw a man and woman silhouetted in the dim light filtering through the old beveled sidelights. They were locked in each other's embrace. Stephanie backed away, her heart in her throat, suppressing the sob that threatened to erupt.

Stephanie toyed with her breakfast. She had arrived earlier than usual—determined to avoid Lance at any cost. She knew their business relations would have to continue and soon they would be forced to meet. But not just yet—not until she had had time to make peace with her sorrow.

Stephanie didn't blame Lance. After all, she had set terms that he couldn't accept. But how could he go straight from her arms to those of another woman if he loved her?

She shuddered and reached for her coffee cup. Its warmth felt good to her cold hands.

Deep in thought, Stephanie failed to see the door open and a tall man, light catching the burnished copper lights in his thick hair, slip in behind her. She picked up her fork and pushed the food around her plate.

"I thought you looked like you were losing weight. Now I know why!"

Stephanie jumped and turned toward the voice behind her. His eyes were warm and merry, but concern played in them, too.

She flushed and dropped her head, not willing to meet his eyes.

"Have you added not speaking to me to your list, Stephanie? I know you've been avoiding me lately."

She managed an off-handed shrug and remarked, "We've both been busy."

"I know, dear," Lance remarked. "You've performed a miracle getting this place back in shape after the storm."

Stephanie flinched at the endearing term. With studied determination she kept her voice steady. "I didn't do it by myself. Abby's help was invaluable."

"Steph, I came early on purpose, hoping I could catch you. We've got to talk."

Stephanie faced him squarely, a shield of indifference turning her eyes gray. "Yes, we need to discuss several things—business matters."

"Yes, that too."

She smiled coolly, "What can I help you with?"

"Get that cold look off your face for one thing! This is Lance, remember?"

"Oh, yes, I remember," she replied ever so softly, her

eyes still hooded.

Lance sighed, then spoke in short clipped tones, anger evident in the clinch of his jaw. "I don't know how much time you've had to study, but we start shooting your scenes next week. We'll go over your part as soon as you feel comfortable with it. It'll have to be at night or early morning, since I'll be tied up during the day."

"Fine. Do you think it'll be necessary for you to take up your time with me? It's just a small part."

"Don't you understand? I want to."

"No, I don't."

For a moment, Lance's familiar impudent grin broke the grimness of his countenance. "Just say my professional judgment is at stake here. The part is small, but it's vital to the picture."

Her face closed tighter against him. "I see. Whenever and wherever, you just let me know. Now I'd really better get busy."

Stephanie half-rose from her chair. Lance's hand shot out and grabbed her arm, forcing her back into her chair. "Stephanie, I think this has gone far enough."

"What's gone far enough?"

"This Ice Maiden bit. You've avoided me, and now you act like we're strangers. I don't like it. In fact, I won't have it. What's happened to us?"

"Don't you know, Lance?"

"I know you gave me some silly ultimatum that I can't live up to, but we can work that out."

"With Alana?"

"With Alana—what do you mean by that?"

"Like sharing your quarters with her?"

"My what? You mean you think—"

"What else could I think?"

Lance narrowed his eyes and snapped his mouth shut. A muscle twitched in the side of his tense face. Very slowly and precisely he spoke. "You could think I love you and you could trust me. Obviously you have graver reservations about me than I knew. Maybe someday you'll find someone worthy of you, Miss. Haynes—but you'll *never* find a man who loves you more."

Lance stood up abruptly and moved resolutely toward the door. Then as an afterthought, he said over his shoulder, "Abby talked to me last week about the need for additional staff. Do whatever you think best. From now on you make all the decisions concerning Boulder Bay. I'll be too busy with the film. If you need additional money in the account, let me know."

Stephanie sat motionless, staring straight ahead. In an instant, Lance was gone, and the door slammed behind him with a sense of finality that broke her heart. His outrage—could she be mistaken about Alana? Had she misjudged him, failed to give him the trust he deserved?

Stephanie dropped her head in her hands and pushed her blond hair back with her hand as if she could clear her mind. She had seen them in the dimness of Lance's cottage, and he let Alana live in his cottage—what else could it be? Stephanie shook her head. There *was* no other explanation. How could he expect her to believe anything else?

For all Lance's good intentions and finely tuned scheduling, weeks passed and still he had not called for the filming of Stephanie's scene. She avoided the set but picked up bits and pieces about mysterious production problems involving both equipment and crew. Even the usually cooperative leading lady seemed destined to delay production. Gossip had it that she spent too many hours in the hotel casino and was too tired to remember her lines.

On rare occasions when Stephanie ran into Lance, his face was lined with fatigue. Dark circles shadowed his eyes. She never saw him laugh, and she heard the crew talk about the boss' short temper.

A brilliant fall had come and gone. The winds had a winter chill in them and the trees had dropped their leaves, but Stephanie had been too busy by day and too troubled by night to note the passing seasons. One thing she did notice—the film was weeks behind schedule. When winter arrived in all its fury, outside filming would have to be suspended. The scenes scheduled for completion by late fall would have to be rescheduled for spring.

Stephanie ached for Lance. When she saw him across the crowded dining room, she wanted to take her hands and smooth away the tired lines, to make him laugh, to see the warm, merry lights shine in his eyes again.

Alana no longer lived in Lance's bungalow. Shortly after the storm repairs were finished, Abby enhanced one of the cottages according to the star's detailed instructions. It had been expensive, but necessary. Abby said Alana had objected fiercely every time the office was used, so Lance had directed Abby to fix Alana a place that suited her— whatever the cost.

Abby laughed when she told Stephanie. "Just think what a drawing card that cottage will be. We can charge three times as much to rent it. It's very plush, and Alana ended up paying for most of the cost. I don't know how Lance managed that, but he did. Too bad he can't manage her on the set as well—but then who could? I'd never heard she was so difficult to work with. You know, I've been helping her with her lines and she couldn't be sweeter, but does she ever give Lance a hard time. Complains all the time about this dull hamlet—says she's dying of boredom."

Stephanie bit her lip and frowned. "You know I've had dinner with her several times. She's always been real pleasant to me. Have you ever noticed her eyes, Abby?"

"They're large and beautiful, is that what you mean?"

"No. When she's off guard, there's a sadness in them. Almost wistful, a little childlike. Sometimes I feel like she needs protecting, that she's vulnerable."

"Well, that's a charitable reaction to her I dare say. I wish I had your forgiving spirit."

"As far as I know, she's done nothing to need my forgiveness."

"She and Lance—"

"I really don't know about that. Sometimes I wonder—"

"If you weren't too hasty?"

"Yeah. It's just, who could resist her? They've known each other a long time, you know."

"That's right, and if Lance had wanted Alana DeLue, he's had ample opportunity to get her before Stephanie Haynes ever appeared in the picture."

"What you say makes a lot of sense, Abby. I'd find it easier if only I hadn't—" Stephanie stopped, not willing to share what she had seen in the darkness on Lance's porch.

"Only what?" Abby probed gently.

"Nothing. What I think is no longer the problem. Lance has decided our differences are irreconcilable. Perhaps he's right. Better to find out now rather than later."

Stephanie plopped down on the sofa. "I do wish I could help him some way with all these production problems."

Abby wrinkled her nose. "Short of straightening out Alana, I don't know what would help. All these minor accidents and delays seem so strange. Everything went like clockwork while the restoration work was underway, but as soon as the movie started, everything went haywire. I surely wouldn't want to be in Lance's shoes. It must be costing him a mint!"

Stephanie nodded her head in agreement as cold fear clutched her heart. Lance had risked his future on this film; what if he failed? She shook her head, rejecting the thought. Lance never failed at anything.

A week later Lance met Stephanie in her office.

"Stephanie, you're aware of my problems—we're way behind schedule. Somehow my leading lady just can't get it together. She seems to be unhappy here, so she's going to fly back to Hollywood for a break."

"Why do you put up with that, Lance? Can't you replace her? Surely you could find another actress who would do as well?"

"That isn't an option. You know she's a major investor. I had hoped to run a tight ship and use as little of her money as possible so I would retain full control of the venture, but because of these delays, I'm about to run out of the money that I and the other small investors had put into the deal. If I replace Alana, I'll lose her backing and won't be able to finish the film. Needless to say, I'll be ruined, and the others will lose their investments. I don't want that to happen!"

Stephanie looked up at him, her eyes full of pain.

Lance, misinterpreting her look, chuckled bitterly.

"Don't worry about Boulder Bay. You should be fine. As long as we keep the location here, the income from that will make the inn self-supporting. I don't have any more capital to invest in the improvements, though."

Stephanie bit her lip, hurt that Lance thought her only concern was the future of Boulder Bay. She replied coolly, "I see. Boulder Bay can make it financially, but if you need your investment back—well, that's another story."

Lance's eyes hardened and he spoke curtly. "That isn't a consideration. I didn't even imply that. I'm going to be fine and so is this movie. I'll see to that. I really came over here to tell you that I have restructured the filming schedule to work around Alana's scenes."

"How much of her footage do you have?"

"Usable footage? Zilch!"

"Is this the first time you've worked with her?"

"No. In the past she has been completely cooperative. Oh, she demanded her status symbols as a star, but on the set, she was totally professional."

Stephanie frowned, puzzled. "Do you have any idea what her problem is?"

Lance nodded. "I think so. She lost her husband tragically eighteen months ago. She almost went off the deep end. Maybe she's not ready to handle the stress." He sighed, discouragement bleeding though his determined countenance.

"Well if she's not, maybe she'll voluntarily relinquish her part," Stephanie probed, seeking to find a solution to Lance's problems and restore the jaunty self-confidence that usually sparkled in his eyes.

"No, I had a long talk with her today. No luck. I hope her trip will help."

"I hope so, too, Lance." Genuine concern lighted Stephanie's eyes. "Now what about the new schedule?"

"Oh yes. Almost forgot why I came. Meet me tonight downstairs where you made your screen test, and we'll go over your part until you're comfortable with it. We'll start your filming tomorrow."

The fear Stephanie had expected with this announcement didn't materialize. Her main concern was assisting Lance. "Fine," she said. "I'm ready."

Lance studied her a moment and smiled. His eyes lingered on her briefly with a touch of the old tenderness in them. "You amaze me, Stephanie Haynes. With all your other duties, you're still prepared."

Her lips curved slightly upward, her eyes soft in response. "Anything for you, Lance."

Stephanie was waiting, script in hand, when Lance arrived, fifteen minutes late. He shot her a look of apology as he rushed in, removing his tie and unbuttoning his collar. "I took Alana to the plane. The drive is farther than I realized. Are you ready?"

Stephanie raised an eyebrow. "Where is Doug? Isn't he going to read his part?"

"No, I'm going to, but we're going to do more than read. I want to make sure you have the movements right."

"How can you watch and act at the same time?"

"I just have a feeling about this. Let's get into position."

For the next two hours, Lance gave Stephanie acting lessons. Masterfully he pulled from her inner being joy or sorrow, agitation or exhilaration. With a natural ability she didn't know she possessed, she conveyed a mood with the blink of an eye or the flick of her hand.

When they approached the final scene, Lance was jubilant. Stephanie had surpassed his expectations. Tomorrow the cameras would roll and discover a new star.

By his direction she turned her back to him and began her lines. This was the parting love scene.

Stephanie began the lines softly, emotion and pain reflected in her voice. Lance walked up behind her and, placing both hands on her shoulders, turned her around slowly and pulled her into the circle of his arms.

Tears streamed down Stephanie's face as she spoke the parting words of the script. Lance stared intensely into her face, responding softly, pleading. Finally, with pain and anger blazing in his eyes, he crushed her to him in a defiant kiss.

Stephanie shuddered and tried to push away from him as the script directed, but Lance only tightened his hold. His kiss lingered, and suddenly Stephanie forgot the script. She felt the sanctuary of Lance's arms around her, the warmth of his lips on hers, remembered the joy of their earlier shared moments. Her arms moved up around his neck. All resistance ceased as she returned his kiss.

When Lance finally raised his head, his breathing was ragged, his eyes bright. He searched her face, caressing it with his eyes. "Steph?"

She moved her fingers, pressed them gently against his mouth, and shook her head. "Not now, Lance. I can't think straight."

He gave a low throaty laugh. "You think too much. I told you—follow your heart."

She shook her head once more, agony in her eyes. "It has to be head and heart, Lance."

He dropped his arms down by his side and stepped away,

a bitter smile on his face. "Love involves compromise, Stephanie. Since you're not willing to give a little, perhaps you *are* following your heart."

Stephanie flinched at his caustic tone, but she replied firmly, "That's why I can't compromise on some issues, Lance. I love you too much to see you miserable. Don't you understand? Love is for a lifetime. I'm afraid we don't have enough building blocks to make it last. Anything less, I'm not willing to settle for."

Lance stared at Stephanie and said harshly, "I understand. I don't measure up to your preconceived notions of what a man is supposed to be. Very well, Miss. Haynes. May I congratulate you? You play a love scene exceptionally well."

Stephanie's face flushed with anger and pain. "Thank you, Mr. Director. That's what you're paying me to do, isn't it?"

Lance clamped his jaw together, setting his mouth in a hard line and giving her a mock salute. "Touché, my dear. At least my professional judgment has been vindicated."

Stephanie moaned, "Oh Lance. Stop it. Why are we saying these things to each other? I don't want to hurt you. I told you that. Remember?"

"Oh, yes, I remember," he replied softly.

"Then what's happened?"

"I made an error in judgment."

Stephanie stepped back as if he'd slapped her. An icy mask shielded Lance's blue eyes, and the man she knew and loved removed himself from her reach.

She took a deep breath and spoke calmly, her voice flat. "I'm sorry you feel that way, Lance. I so wanted you to understand."

A knock interrupted her, and a tall, handsome young man in his early thirties opened the door and walked in. He glanced uncertainly from Lance to Stephanie as Lance barked, "Yes?"

The young man smiled broadly, showing even white teeth beneath his close-cut, dark mustache. "I was looking for Stephanie Haynes, and I think I've just found her." His large brown eyes crinkled with pleasure as he gave her a warm, appreciative look.

Stephanie stared at him without responding. There was something familiar about this handsome stranger. Something in his mannerisms that drew her, but her mind, so filled with Lance, refused to place him.

By this time he was crossing the room, his eyes glued to hers. "Stephanie Haynes, the ravages of time have been generous with you. The pretty little girl is a beauty who takes my breath away!"

A joyous exclamation broke from Stephanie, and she rushed forward to meet him with outstretched arms. "Todd!" she managed before all sight and sounds were muffled in a rib-crushing embrace that lifted her off her feet.

"I can't believe it. Where, when, how?" she babbled unintelligently as he laughed freely.

"I told you I'd be back."

"Yes, but that was so long ago." She leaned her head back, still encircled by his arms, and added softly, "So very long ago."

Behind her Lance stirred, remarking, "Stephanie, I suppose that'll be all."

She whirled from Todd, her face pink with embarrassment, her eyes alight with excitement.

"Oh, excuse me, Lance. This is an old childhood friend. Todd Andrews, meet Lance Donovan, my...my partner and...my boss."

"If you can be her boss, you must be a rare individual. Unless this girl has changed, she's a handful."

Lance took the outstretched hand and remarked sardonically, "She hasn't changed a bit."

Stephanie spoke quickly. "Lance is a movie producer and director. He's filming a movie here at Boulder Bay."

Todd nodded his head. "Yes, I know. That's why I'm here. Your assistant wrote me and told me everything that was going on here and some of your needs. I just couldn't resist coming to see for myself."

Lance moved toward the door and spoke amiably. "Good meeting you, Andrews, but I have an early call in the morning. If you two will excuse me, I'll leave you to catch up on old times."

As he passed Stephanie, Lance remarked, "Don't stay up too late. I don't want the makeup lady to have to cover all that natural beauty trying to get out fatigue lines."

Stephanie searched Lance's face. His nonchalant manner conveyed indifference, and the vibrant eyes that had glowed with love and tenderness now looked at her with the coolness of a casual acquaintance. She ached for her loss.

eleven

Despite Lance's warning, Stephanie and Todd sat in the old kitchen replete with childhood memories and talked, filling in the long years that had separated them.

Martha sat with them for several hours, and her matchmaking bent couldn't resist asking the handsome young lawyer about the governor's daughter. Todd responded with the sad story of two people from different worlds who held conflicting values. The experience left him leery of politics and skeptical of women.

Todd reached out and took Stephanie's hand, adding, "I needed to come home to lick my wounds. And when I thought of home, I thought of you, Stephanie. You're the nearest thing to a family I have left, so when Abby called, I came running home to you."

A lump swelled in Stephanie's throat as the longing and pain of the past weeks rushed out. "Oh, Todd. I need you so. We all do."

Todd leaned over and, too overcome with emotion to speak, took Stephanie in his arms, and she began to sob on his shoulder. She rested in the haven of his arms as the emotional storm buffeted her, providing an overdue and much-needed release.

Todd patted the blond head on his shoulder and stroked the long silken hair that streamed down her back. They sat thus until the sobbing subsided. The young attorney lifted Stephanie's chin and wiped away the trail of tears and smeared mascara that ran down her cheeks. Placing a light kiss on her forehead, he teased, "You look like a blue-eyed raccoon, Stephanie."

With a sigh, Todd continued his story. "The decision hurt; I won't say that it didn't. But marriage is for a lifetime. Our differences were so basic that a marriage wouldn't have endured. I fully believe God closed the door for me in Texas. And, if He did, then I know He has something better for me.

"I just hope it isn't politics," he added with a wry smile, his arm still cradling Stephanie. "Maybe it's here. Emerald Cove is a long way from state house politics. Just a simple country lawyer in a community with traditional values is what I'm looking to be. I'm excited about the things Abigail has told me."

"Now that Abigail, she's a *real* girl. One that'd make any man proud," Martha interrupted.

Stephanie and Todd burst into relief-giving laughter. Martha, the irrepressible matchmaker, was at work again.

"By the way, Martha, how did Abigail know about Todd?"

"Um, er, we were talking one day, and I sort of mentioned Todd, and then later on she asked me about him again. And you know Abby. The next thing I knew, Todd was standing on the doorstep. Not that I mind a bit, you know," Martha explained, nodding her head for emphasis. She reached over and patted Todd's hand reassuringly.

"I know that, Martha. You've always had a knack for making me feel welcome."

"That's because you are."

"That means more than I could ever tell you, especially since I lost my parents. It's real strange—Stephanie and I both being all alone in the world. Guess you and John are going to have to be our folks." Todd grinned infectiously at Martha, and she blushed while unspoken appreciation glowed in her eyes.

"Nothing John and I would like better. It's like having children of our own, having Abby and Stephanie in the house." Then her face clouded and she added as an afterthought, "But mind you, me and John won't live forever. You need to be making a home of your own. Maybe have a few babies these old arms could rock."

She stopped, embarrassed that she had revealed her innermost longings.

"You've got plenty of time for that, Martha. And don't you worry. Someday I plan to have a houseful, and you'll be so busy rocking, you'll wear the rockers off your chairs," Todd declared.

"Who's going to have a houseful of what?" called Abby as she bounded down the back stairs, her crimson robe setting off her dark beauty, and her eyes sparkling with the excitement of life.

"Me. Don't I look like the fatherly type?" Todd asked with a grin.

"Is this something that's supposed to be immediate?" Abby teased.

"There're a few other items on the agenda first," he confessed.

"I'm relieved to hear that, Mr. Attorney! If you decide to stay here, we're going to have you so busy you'll not have time for outside activities. Look at Stephanie and me—we're strictly working girls."

"That's sure true, and if I might add a word, I think it's a shame," Martha said, her lips in a disapproving line.

"Yeah, I can see all work and no play has made them dull girls." With a laugh at Abigail who made a face at him, Todd added, "You leave them to Uncle Todd, Martha. I'll have these two straightened out before you know it. They just need a firm hand. You've spoiled them."

Abby nodded her head, "That's a fact."

Her exuberance dispelled the last vestige of sadness, and the three young people continued a merry exchange for several hours after Martha had retired to her quarters. Stephanie and Todd entertained Abigail with childhood tales of their misadventures. She laughed until tears streamed down her cheeks.

As the wall clock chimed three times, Stephanie jumped up from the table, exclaiming, "Lance Donovan will have my hide. I'm afraid I'll be forced to leave this stimulating company."

"If you think you must. I'm just getting started. It's two hours earlier in Texas, you know," Todd reminded.

"Well, don't wear Abby out, Todd. She's not on Texas time either."

"I'll be on up in a little while, Steph. You'd better get a couple of cold cucumber slices to put on your eyes. Lance won't like a red, puffy-eyed starlet;" Abby commanded.

Stephanie placed the back of her hand on her forehead and gave a mock frown. "Oh, what sacrifices we must make to preserve our beauty. But then, that's show biz."

She exited with the gentle laughter of her friends following her up the stairs. For the first time in weeks, Stephanie felt relaxed. For a few moments, her heart had thrown off its pain, and the brooding face of Lancelot Donovan had not haunted her every thought. In the shelter of Todd's arms, she had felt warmth and protection.

The hour was late, but the evening had been therapeutic. Yes, she hoped Todd stayed. She breathed a silent prayer, *Please, God, I need him.*

Stephanie's first session before the camera went smoothly, and her self-confidence grew. Her hardest adjustment had been her audience.

Since she had spent little time observing the film crew at work, she didn't realize so many people were involved in the process. Not only the actors, but stand-ins stood by as the makeup and wardrobe people hurried to and fro with touch-ups and assistance readily available. Along with Abigail and Todd, several crew members stood on the sidelines observing. Stephanie suspected they were curious about their hostess-turned-actress, but their faces revealed they were here to cheer her on.

Her mind wandered for a moment before she realized a hush had come over the set. Lance walked up and curtly asked the bystanders to move back and the actors to take their places. He, too, had noticed the size of the audience, and his face registered disapproval.

Stephanie walked to the center to meet Douglas McNeil, the young man who would play her love interest. She smiled at him, genuine affection crinkling her eyes. If ever a man met the criteria of a romantic hero, Doug did. He stood tall, blond, and handsome, like a hero from a Viking epic. His every movement flowed with masculine grace and magnetism. Lance had, once again, chosen his character with great care.

Stephanie had just inquired about the health of Doug's wife when Lance curtly interrupted, "Miss Haynes, if you and Doug are finished with your conversation, I believe we need to get started."

Stephanie looked up into the cool eyes of the director and replied calmly, "We're quite finished, thank you. What would you have us do?"

"We'll begin with the scene at the front door."

Stephanie nodded and obediently turned to the make-shift door. Her first experience as a professional actress began.

Soon she forgot everything except her part, the hero, and the director barking orders. Lance no longer was her Lance, but rather someone whose command she instantly obeyed as he fine-tuned her performance. He skillfully brought her through the scene several times, and shortly before lunch, the cameras rolled, recording Stephanie's first scene.

When it was over, they became Lance and Stephanie again, and her heart yearned to know he had approved. She watched him covertly to see if she could gauge his feelings about her performance. She couldn't. After his first curt words to her, his attitude had been one of impeccable professional aloofness. While they had been filming, she relished his professionalism; now she longed for that intimate smile that told her she was special, that he'd been pleased. It was not forthcoming.

Lance had patiently explained what he wanted and at times had walked through the scene with her. There was no difference between the way he treated her and Doug. His explanations were explicit, and he expected them to be followed. They were. He had not boasted vainly of his abilities. He was good at his job. Stephanie marveled at his communication skills and wondered why he'd had so much trouble with Alana. Surely an experienced actress would appreciate and respond to his outstanding ability.

The crew broke for lunch, and Stephanie headed toward her friends. Suddenly she felt hungry. Breakfast had been scant. She'd been too excited to eat.

Abby praised her abundantly. Todd reached over and gave her an enthusiastic hug and kiss, congratulating her. Stephanie laughed with relief, thankful for her friends and their encouragement. Putting her arm around Todd's waist, she walked buoyantly toward the inn and the meal that awaited.

Unseen by Stephanie, Lance had started toward her until he witnessed the tender scene. To his eyes, it looked more like a reunion between lovers than the affectionate encouragement between friends. His eyes clouded before pain brought down an icy curtain of studied indifference. Perhaps here was the man who could meet Stephanie's standards.

During the next few days, Lance drove Stephanie and Doug unmercifully. He filmed every inch of footage he could, with an eye on the weather. Unseasonable warmth blessed production, so he pressed to complete the outdoor scenes before winter arrived in earnest. He squeezed every moment of progress he could from the daylight hours. After dark, he went inside and perfected each scene for the next day.

Miraculously, the weather held as well as Lance's luck. The earlier problems that had delayed him abated, and he finished all the outdoor scenes the day before the weather broke.

Tension showed in his face, and dark circles deepened under his eyes. He ate his meals on the run and talked little.

Stephanie had a hard time relating this Lance to the easy-going man she had fallen in love with. But she didn't love him any less. The more she worked with him, the more her heart ached.

She longed to smooth his brow, to do something to ease his burden. But even more than that she longed to hear him call her Steph and caress her face with eyes warmed by love.

Instead, Lance remained cool and aloof. As a boss, he couldn't be faulted. As the man she loved, he broke her heart. How could real love change so rapidly to indifference? Her heart wrenched. She didn't want to know the answer.

Todd and Abigail apprehensively watched tension drain the energy from another face and they puzzled. Martha watched too and finally broached the subject. "Stephanie's getting too thin."

"She must be working too hard. I noticed she looks kind of tired. Lance won't like that. He almost gave me a lecture about keeping her up the first night I was here," Todd reasoned.

"Yes, she's working hard. But she's worked hard before," Abigail hedged.

"Yep, that's worried tired, not working tired." Martha tersely observed.

Todd raised his eyebrows inquisitively. "Worried? Worried about what? She seems a real winner in front of the camera, and as for the inn, I've been over the books, and you're covering operating costs and even making a little profit."

"It's not the inn or her acting. It's Lance," Abigail inserted.

"What do you mean, Lance? He seems fair enough and satisfied with her performance."

"It isn't business, it's her heart."

"You mean Stephanie's in love with Lance?"

"I mean they are both in love with each other."

"You must be kidding. He doesn't appear interested in anything but his business. He's a genius in his job, though. I considered him a mighty cold chap, myself. Tried to be friendly to him. He appeared congenial enough, but withdrawn. Are you sure?"

"The Lance you see now is not the real Lance. He shut himself away from everyone behind a wall of determination."

"Why?"

"Two reasons. For one thing the production is in trouble. It's way behind schedule and substantially over budget, not to mention the leading lady has gone AWOL."

"That's too bad, but if it's a success then he'll have no problem with losses."

"That's a big if. You see, Lance put most of his assets into this picture, and he's about out of money. That's why he pushes the crew so hard. He contacted Alana and told her to come back and release some of her funds—she's the other investor. So far she's refused both requests."

Todd gave a low whistle, "No wonder he's worried. If he's out of money and production stops, he'll not be able to finish the picture—"

"And he'll lose the right to the script. One of the conditions was that the film be released next summer. We don't have any usable footage of Alana."

"Well, why doesn't he get other backers and another star?"

"There isn't time, and I don't know if he can get out of his agreement with her."

"Do you think he'd let me look at his contract?"

"I don't think so. Not in the mood he's in right now. He's fighting the inevitable."

"Poor guy. I know the feeling. A man's career is vital to his self-esteem. If I hadn't recognized God's hand in the problems I had in Texas, I don't know how I would have survived it. Looking back, I can see it was the best thing for me. But what does this have to do with Stephanie?"

"It's all wrapped up together. He asked her to marry him, but only after the movie was a success so he could take care of her in royal style."

"What's wrong with that?"

"Men! There's nothing wrong with wanting to, but sometimes things happen that make it impossible. She feels like love is sharing the good times and the bad. He feels a relationship like that makes a man weak. He's very self-sufficient, and I might add, so is Stephanie. They were bound to collide, and now they are both miserable."

"Well, what can we do to fix it?"

"Mr. Fix-it, don't you know there are some things we just can't fix?" Abigail's bright eyes danced merrily.

"Isn't that the pot calling the kettle black?"

Abigail wrinkled her nose thoughtfully. "You've got a point there, counselor."

Todd touched the tip of her nose with his finger and added, "We're a lot alike, you know."

"Oh, no. Batten down the hatches. There'll be trouble ahead," she laughed.

The smile left his face, and he looked steadily into the liquid brown eyes turned up to his. "I think it's enchanting,

Abigail."

His soft drawl gave her name a musical sound, and in his eyes, she could see the memory of a Texas girl fading.

The winter winds howled outside while inside the crew prepared to finish the final scenes they could shoot without Alana.

Guests at the inn watched, fascinated, as the crew worked. Lance proved amazingly cooperative in working around them, and even let some participate as extras, much to their delight.

They shot party scenes in the Victorian parlor and moved to the carriage house to film beside a roaring fire. Meanwhile, Lance's face grew more drawn and haggard. Even the crew began to question the whereabouts of their leading lady.

Lance battled his own private agony with that question. Alana had refused to come back, and only one scene was left to shoot without her. He mulled over a million options, but none of them proved viable. He was out of time and money.

His last call to Alana proved futile. She didn't relish the cold weather, so neither the money nor Alana arrived. Threats and pleading accomplished nothing. *If she didn't cooperate soon*—he couldn't finish the thought. He clinched his fist tight, and a tiny muscle twitched in his jaw. He'd find a way, he always had. Somehow, too much was at stake: his career and maybe Stephanie.

A bitter smile played at the corner of Lance's mouth. No, not Stephanie. He had lost her already. He closed his eyes, and images of her intruded. He saw her thin and pale. She had lost weight recently, but it only enhanced her beautiful features. Her confidence had improved, and now she projected on screen that inner radiance which had captivated him from the first moment he'd seen her. If things were different, he'd be jubilant with his discovery, but unless Alana came through, the world would never experience Stephanie's radiance and beauty.

Lance knew with proper management Stephanie could become a star who would far exceed the Alanas in the industry. He cringed inwardly. What would stardom do to her? Would it destroy the very radiance that made her unique? He thought not, but it wasn't worth the chance. She was too special, too innocent.

He growled and tried to thrust her from his mind. He had not allowed himself this indulgence in weeks; not since the night Todd had arrived. He was probably the reason she looked thin and pale, too many late nights catching up on old times. Well, he'd warned her.

Suddenly his mind burned with the memory of that night. In a few minutes he would leave to direct the scene they had rehearsed. He'd watch her in the arms of another man, but he'd be remembering how she'd felt in his arms, the sweet fragrance of her hair, the warmth of her response. He whirled and slammed the wall with his fist, his tightly controlled indifference dissolved.

A knock interrupted and a voice informed him that the set waited. Lance took a deep breath and squared his shoulders. A scowl darkened his face as he walked out his door and toward the cottage where the crew waited. Determination to put memories aside set his face like a flint.

He cleared the set of visitors and sent the makeup and wardrobe women away. There would be no audience today. No curious eyes would observe this scene.

The tension in Lance transmitted itself to the set, and for the first time, Stephanie had trouble with her lines.

After many attempts, Lance abruptly called for an hour's break, and remarked scathingly to Stephanie, "Maybe you can learn your lines by then."

Stephanie flushed, but she looked directly in his eyes until he returned her gaze. "I did learn these lines," she said softly. "I knew them earlier, remember?"

Lance turned on his heel and stalked away without answering, but not before Stephanie saw his mask of icy indifference slip, revealing the pain beneath. Somehow it comforted her.

During the break, Stephanie didn't study her lines. She studied her heart and her reluctance to play the scene. Forcibly, she recalled that night weeks ago when Lance had held her. She experienced once again every emotion that had engulfed her. When she finished, she walked back to the set, ready to begin. Out of her reservoir of memories, she would play the scene with the power and pathos it deserved.

Soft firelight reflected on the warm cherry walls of the cottage. A man and woman stood at the door, encased in the aura.

Her face, translucent in the firelight, glowed with a love that revealed her soul, yet in her eyes an agony of pain blazed. Her voice spoke soft words of a final farewell.

The blond giant gathered her tenderly into his arms and wiped away the tears that streamed down her face. Then lowering his head, he claimed her lips in a long, gentle kiss. The camera moved in and captured the face of the woman as it revealed the gamut of her emotions from sheer ecstasy to agonizing despair.

The shoot ended with a fade-out of the woman's wide blue eyes looking up into the face of her beloved. A hushed silence followed, only broken when the director's husky voice pronounced it a take.

Without a word, Lance left the room, the door slamming forlornly behind him. Spontaneously, everyone broke into applause. Stephanie tried to respond, but finding she couldn't speak, she simply nodded in appreciation to her friends as she, too, turned and walked away.

For those few moments it had been Lance who held her. There had been no cameras for her, no other people present, only the memory of his arms, the pain and ecstasy of that night. Now it was captured on film for the world to see. She sighed, glad it was over.

The days grew shorter as winter tightened its hold on the New England countryside. Winds blew in from the sea, biting and stinging all who dared to venture outdoors.

Stephanie watched and waited, but Alana did not return. Lance spent his time in the basement workrooms going over the footage they had completed. Had he been on schedule, he would have been ecstatic with what they had shot. Unfortunately, without the leading lady and her scenes, they only had bits and pieces of a collage.

He smothered his distress by perfecting what he had. Little by little, his aloofness thawed, and he joined the group in a game of Scrabble or lively conversation. He looked morose, but the fatigue lines eased, and Stephanie knew he must be getting more rest.

Their relationship improved. They now discussed

business, the inn, its potential. The suggestions Lance gave Stephanie for the coming holidays resulted in a large number of reservations for Thanksgiving.

Stephanie relished the opportunity to talk to Lance. Despite the congenial companionship of her friends, she missed him. Todd and Abigail were efficient and thorough when it came to business, but neither possessed Lance's foresight and creativity.

One afternoon, the distant sound of jingling bells drew Stephanie to the front window. Her eyes rounded in bewilderment as a horse-drawn sled pulled up in front of the porch. She laughed when Todd leaped out and bounded up the porch. "Todd, there's barely a half inch of snow out there. Aren't you pushing the season a bit?"

Todd's face fell, but his eyes held their excitement. "I just couldn't help it, Steph. Lance told me to find one, and I did. An old farmer in Bay Side had what we needed, so I went after it. You get bundled up. We're all going for a ride."

Todd went in search of Lance, and soon four bundled-up adults arrived on the porch anxious for the new adventure. Todd sat in the driver's seat as Stephanie moved to the back seat. Lance climbed in beside her. Puzzled, he looked from Stephanie to Todd but said nothing. He helped Abigail in beside Todd, and the sled glided over the icy layer of snow while the foursome laughed and talked like children.

The wind grew steadily stronger, and Stephanie shivered, pulling her stocking cap down farther over her curls. Lance placed his arm protectively around her, and she nestled in the curve of his shoulder, putting her face down on his chest and away from the stinging wind.

Lance's arm tightened, and Stephanie could hear the thundering of his heart. A longing to recapture the precious moments of last summer flooded her. Memory transported her back to when their lives were filled with the rapture of simply being together, before the conflicts and questions began. She felt so warm in Lance's arms, so safe and protected. So complete.

Darkness came too swiftly for Stephanie. Before she was willing, the sled arrived back at the inn's front door. When Lance handed the girls out of the sled, Stephanie noticed he treated Abigail with the same warm courtesy as he did her. Perhaps she'd been mistaken about the flicker of pain in his eyes, the thundering of his heart.

Stephanie gave Lance a shy smile. If she couldn't have his love, she'd cherish his friendship. He winked in return, and for the first time in weeks, the old Lance peeked out from behind his troubled countenance.

twelve

Lance sent the crew home for Thanksgiving and told them they could stay on through Christmas unless they heard from him. Stephanie knew he'd given up on Alana's return, and she waited for the inevitable, wishing he'd talk to her.

After the sleigh ride, Lance had seemed in better spirits, a fact which mystified Stephanie. One night the foursome decided to go into town for a movie. Once again, Lance looked puzzled when Abigail took the seat next to Todd in the car, but he made no comment. The movie turned out to be one of Lance's, and he balked at going in, but his friends dragged him, laughing and protesting, into the theater.

Walking from the auditorium afterward, Stephanie impulsively took Lance's hand and squeezed it, her eyes bright and moist. "Lance, you're so good at your job. I wish all movies left you feeling uplifted like that."

He stopped and turned to her. With a strange light in his eyes, he searched her face. Then he frowned and faced forward. Still holding her hand, he placed it in the crook of his arm before replying, "I'm glad you liked it."

For the rest of the evening, Lance remained subdued. They headed for the coffee shop, the college crowd's usual hangout which for once was deserted. Todd challenged Stephanie to find some suitable music on the jukebox. She took the challenge, and pulling Todd after her, left Lance and Abby at the table alone.

Abby stood the gloomy silence as long as she could, "Lance Donovan, will you tell me what's the matter with you?"

"I've got a lot on my mind. Some big decisions to make."

"I know. But what happened in the movie tonight?"

"It just reminded me of what I'm facing."

"What, Lance?"

"Losing my career."

"You're not going to lose your career," Abby protested.

"Yes, I am, Abby. Tonight's film reminded me of what I stand to lose in my career, not to mention. . . ." and he nodded his head toward Stephanie.

"Lance, don't be foolish. Stephanie loves you."

"What about him?"

"Todd?" Abby asked, incredulity written on her pert features.

"Yes, Todd. He's a fine man with all the characteristics that Stephanie's looking for in a man."

"That's right, but she isn't in love with Todd. He is like a big brother to her. It's you she loves, you big lug."

"Aside from all that, our other differences are too great."

"Can't you change a little?"

"Maybe, but if I change just to please her, it won't work, and I refuse to be a hypocrite for her or anyone."

Tears brightened Abby's brown eyes, and she reached over to pat her friend's hand. "Stephanie wouldn't want you to. She told me as much."

"What did she tell you?"

"That she'd never want you to change your mind just to please her. Change must come only because you believe it for yourself. Now what about your career, Lance?"

"I can't give it up. I had decided to walk away from it, find something else to do. Without Stephanie, I thought success didn't matter any more, but I realized tonight it does. I can't walk away. It's my life and I'm good at it. Somehow, I'll find a way to finish this film—I will finish it."

"Can't walk away from what, Lance? Making movies or success?"

"Isn't it the same thing?"

"No. One has to do with purpose, the other ambition."

"You, too, Abby?"

"Me, too, what?"

"Think we have some purpose we were born to, or God created us for as Stephanie put it."

"As a matter of fact, I *know* it."

"How can you know it?"

Abby laughed ruefully. "I guess you could call it trial and error."

Silently, his blue-gray eyes questioned.

"I had my life mapped out," Abby explained. "I didn't consult God about His plans for it, and He allowed me to fall on my face to get my attention."

"That doesn't sound much like the loving God Stephanie talks about."

"On the contrary," Abby disputed. "He wants what is best for us. When we suffer defeats, that's His way of protecting us from a decision that would lead to a miserable or unproductive life."

"I wouldn't say I've had an unproductive life, and I've never consulted Him."

"Maybe up till now you've sort of stumbled on the same

path He'd have you take."

"Up until now?"

"Well, you're having some second thoughts, aren't you?"

"You think God's interested in helping me out of this mess?" Lance asked with a mirthless chuckle.

"Maybe." Abby's eyes flared with sympathy. Her voice hesitated as she weighed her words.

Lance rushed on with a compelling need to share his feelings. "I truly wish I could believe that, but I can't think something like this would matter to Him."

"Lance, it's not the 'something like this' that matters to God."

He shot her an inquisitive glance. "Then what does?"

"It's you, Lance. Lancelot Donovan matters to God. Sometimes He lets us suffer defeats before we can learn that. I can't promise He'll pull this deal out of the fire for you—I wish I could." Abby paused, her brown eyes pleading for his understanding. "He won't if it's not the best thing for you."

Lance shook his head obstinately. "There's no way failing in this could benefit me or anyone else. I'm sorry, Abby. I don't buy it. Failure and defeat can never be anything but bad."

"Lance," her voice and her eyes pleaded with him. "He *can* turn our defeats into victory when we give Him our lives and determine to follow his direction, no matter what."

"That's what bothers me about all this, Abby. I believe God's given us enough equipment to run our lives without bothering Him."

"I know, Lance. I thought that, too, until I ended up in

some situations I couldn't handle."

"You seem pretty happy now."

She laughed. "That's because I found out that God knows how to run my life better than I do."

Lance smiled in response, warm wistfulness touching his eyes. "You sound like Stephanie. I wish I could believe what you said was true, but the way I see it, I got myself into this situation, and I'll have to get myself out."

"What if you can't, Lance?"

"I will, somehow."

"What if you have to compromise your principles?"

Lance sighed deeply. "I'll have to face that when and if the time comes."

Abby impulsively reached over and patted Lance's hand with an encouraging smile. "When the time comes, and it will, I know you will make the right decision."

Lance's eyes brightened. "Thanks, Abby, for that vote of confidence. It felt good to talk to somebody."

Abby cocked her head toward Stephanie who was returning to the table and added, "As for her, you aren't going to lose her. You two were made for each other."

Memory of a warm summer night and Stephanie in his arms flooded Lance and he winced. "I remember saying that to her on a lovely evening a thousand light years ago."

Lance stood up and pulled out a chair for Stephanie as she reached the table. Their eyes collided, his were open and vulnerable while hope dawned in hers.

The ride home was quiet. Just before Todd turned off the main road where the lane began, Lance moved his arm to the back of the seat, his hand resting lightly on Stephanie's shoulder. Suddenly she felt his eyes on her. Lifting her head slowly, she turned toward him. His head was bent down to hers, their lips almost touching. Even in the dimness, she could see his eyes filled with pain and longing.

Without thinking, she put her hand to his cheek, caressing it as she whispered his name. She felt his warm breath on her cheek and then his lips claimed hers. Gently, ever so gently at first, his kiss told her what his words had been reluctant to express. Stephanie's arms crept around Lance's neck, as her lips responded with her own heart's message.

Suddenly his arms swept around her, pulling her to him in a close embrace. The wool of his top coat scratched her face, and she reveled in the smell of his aftershave mingled with wood smoke from the night's walk in town. Her heart thundered as his kiss turned from gentle to intense. His lips told her that he never wanted to let her go; hers pliant beneath his answered in kind. Their desperate embrace spoke of an uncertain future, but their lips proclaimed a love that had past and present.

When Lance finally released Stephanie, the inn was in view. Both were so overcome with pent-up emotion that neither could speak until Todd drove up in front of Lance's cottage.

"Okay, Donovan, here's your lodging. You're back all in one piece thanks to the superb driving skill of one Todd Andrews, not to mention an evening of delightful entertainment. Now what could you find in Hollywood that would top this?"

Lance took Stephanie's hand and kissed her fingertips out of Todd's view. Looking straight into her eyes, he answered, "Not anywhere this side of heaven could I find anything to top this."

Todd cocked an eye in the rearview mirror and retorted,

"Now you don't have to get carried away. I know I'm a lot of fun but. . . ." His retort died as his eyes met Lance's.

Lance turned to Stephanie once again. "Stephanie, would you get out and stay a few minutes? We could have a cup of hot chocolate—or something."

Stephanie smiled reluctantly and shook her head. "I don't think it would be wise, tonight. Could I have a rain check?"

Disappointment sharpened Lance's features. "Sure, anytime."

Stephanie touched Lance's cheek again, creating privacy with her soft voice. "Don't, Lance. We need time to think. The hot chocolate would be fine, but I don't think either of us are up to handling the 'or something.' Do you?"

He looked at her, his eyes dark with emotion, then smiled. "You're right."

Hope and longing transformed Stephanie's features as Lance bid goodnight to his three friends and disappeared behind the cottage door.

The Thanksgiving weekend passed in a flurry of activity, leaving Lance and Stephanie no time to talk. Many of the inn staff had taken the day off, so Abigail, Stephanie, and Todd pitched in to make the holiday a memorable one for their guests. By the end of the day, their ears were ringing with guests' promises of return visits the following year.

Stephanie missed Lance at supper. Abigail told her he had some loose ends to tie up and would get a snack later on. On impulse, Stephanie loaded up a tray with enough leftovers for two and braved the cold wind to carry them to Lance's cottage.

He answered her soft knock at the door with a curt, "It's open."

She pushed against the heavy door and stumbled into the room, a vision of loveliness in her bright red coat and mittens, with eyes shining and cheeks rosy from the cold.

Lance leaped to his feet and took the tray from her. "What did I do to deserve this?"

She wrinkled her nose at him and replied, "Not a thing. I'm hiding out from the chores. You won't give me away will you?"

He chuckled, "What's it worth to you?"

"I brought my bargaining power with me. You see all the goodies on this tray? If you're not good, I'll sit here and eat them all in front of you and not give you a mouthful."

"Now would you treat a poor starving man that way?"

"I might. You can never tell about me."

Their eyes met and held; the lively bantering stopped. "I've missed you, Steph."

She turned quickly from him, her heart in her throat. She shouldn't have come. Those old feelings would engulf her again, and she'd be powerless.

He set the tray down and took her shoulders, turning her to face him. The firelight illumined his features, but his eyes burned from an inner fire. She closed her eyes and shook her head, "I. . .I shouldn't have come. I'd better leave."

"Don't, Stephanie. I need to talk to you. We've wasted so much time. Open your eyes. Look at me," he commanded softly.

She opened her eyes and shook her head. "Nothing has changed. You're still you, I'm still me." Her voice faltered.

Lance pulled Stephanie toward the sofa, and they sat down on its soft pillows. The fire licked at the oak logs and cast long shadows on the wall.

"Why were you sitting in the dark?" Stephanie asked.

"I had a lot to think about, and before I knew it, night had fallen. Now I'm not going to turn on a lamp; you're too beautiful for words, sitting here in the firelight."

"Are you hungry?" she asked as his arm slid down the back of the sofa and cradled her head.

He pressed two fingers against her lips and said, "Shh. Yes, but later. First we'll talk."

"About what?"

"About why you came over here tonight."

"Because I thought you might be hun—"

"The real reason, Stephanie."

Her voice quivered, and her eyes locked in his gaze. "Because I didn't stop to think about it. I just wanted to be with you."

"Thank you," he said.

"For what?"

"Your honesty for one thing. I needed to hear that tonight."

Her eyes, wide and wondering, stared back at him.

"I'm leaving tomorrow."

She nodded her head, pain touching her eyes. "I wondered when you'd be going. Will you be back?"

"Someday."

"Where are you going?"

"To Hollywood. I talked to Alana tonight. She's refused to return, so I'm going to see her and perhaps salvage the film."

"How will you do that?"

"Either by getting her to go through with her agreement or by finding other backers."

"Will you have time before you're option is out?"

He shrugged. "At least I have to try. Completing what we did here will give me a little edge if I don't have to use it up looking for financing. Of course, the best thing is for Alana to go on with it."

"If she doesn't, you'll have to find another actress."

"Yes, but I hope Alana will be more cooperative in Hollywood."

"Do you have any idea why she hasn't been?"

"Who knows? Said she couldn't stand it here. Made her depressed. She told me on the phone that she's ready and eager to get back to work if we can get together on the terms. I can't imagine what she's talking about—other than maybe filming her sequences in California. That'll cost more money since we have the lease here to pay, and we'd have to move everything to California."

"Don't worry about the lease here, Lance."

"Hush, Stephanie. We decided from the beginning that the only way you could make it this year would be with the income from the lease and what you'd make from the movie yourself. I haven't forgotten."

"It's just that I don't want you to worry about us here— if I can't make it, I can't. The inn's worth a lot more now than it was. If I have to sell it, at least you could get your investment back."

"And you'd be left with very little."

"Maybe I could borrow the capital to operate on."

"Too big a financial burden for the inn to carry. No, your survival depends on my honoring our lease, which is one reason I want to get this thing settled. I can't pay you the final installment until Alana or someone comes across with the capital." He squeezed her shoulder reassuringly.

"I didn't realize things were that bad for you, Lance. If you hadn't invested in the inn. . ."

Lance smiled ruefully. "Compared to movie expenses, that's just a drop in the bucket. It would only put off my decision by a few weeks."

She searched his face for the truth. Was he trying to protect her at his expense? She couldn't tell.

"Anyway," Lance continued, "if I'm not successful, this may be the only business venture I have left."

She shuddered. "Don't say that, Lance. You mustn't fail. It means too much to you."

"You're probably right, Steph. It means too much, but that's not what I wanted to talk to you about. I think we need to talk about us."

Her face guarded, she asked, "What about us? Has anything changed?"

"Something has. I'm sharing my problems with you."

"You won't let me help you."

"I don't know how you could."

"Would you if I could?"

He chuckled bitterly. "Probably not."

"Then nothing's changed." Stephanie moved to stand up, but Lance held her back.

"I don't want to quarrel our last night together."

Stephanie dropped her head on his shoulder, shielding her eyes from his probing. "I never want to quarrel with you. It hurts too much. Why do we?"

"Because we're stubborn, and our pride gets in the way. That's one of the things I want to clear up with you before I go."

She raised her head, surprised.

"Do you remember that morning in the kitchen when you suggested I had spent the night with Alana?"

Stephanie bit her lip. Anger briefly flamed in her eyes. "Well, didn't you?"

"No. I have principles, too, Stephanie. That's what angered me, and my pride wouldn't let me explain."

"Then where did you spend your nights?"

"In the unfinished cottage next door. The boys moved a cot over there. That's where I slept. I worked, when Abby was with me, in my office. There was nothing and never has been anything between Alana and me. I wanted you to know that before I went to California to see her."

"But what about that night—"

"What night?"

"I went to your cottage to talk to you about some business, and I saw you and her silhouetted through the door, embracing."

His eyes widened, and then he frowned. "I don't know what you're talking about."

"Lance, it wasn't just a friendly, sympathetic hug. I can recognize passion, even through the door."

His frown disappeared, and he looked at her keenly, then threw back his head and laughed.

Embarrassed, she defended heatedly, "I didn't think it was a laughing matter then, and I don't now."

By the time Lance brought his laughter under control, Stephanie sat primly on the edge of the sofa, her lips pressed together in a tight line.

"Darling, you must be mistaken. I only went in that cottage with Abby, and I never went there after dark."

"I wasn't mistaken, Lance. Now you tell me the whole

truth."

His eyes still danced with amusement. "Believe me, I am. There was no more between Alana and me than between you and Todd."

Stephanie's eyes rounded in surprise, "Todd and me? What are you talking about?"

"For months I labored under the notion that you and Todd had sort of taken up where you'd left off all those years ago. It's plain to see you and he are more. . .er . . .compatible."

"You were jealous, Lance?" Her smile dazzled.

"You could say that," he reluctantly agreed.

"Well, in part you were right. We did take up where we had left off. Todd's the brother I never had."

"So Abby told me."

"And Lance?" Stephanie looked up at him through lowered lashes.

"Yes?"

"There's more to a relationship than compatibility."

"Yeah?" He looked down at her, his eyes dangerously alive.

"Yes, like the sheer joy and excitement in simply being alive that I've felt with you."

"Felt, Stephanie?"

"Feel," she confessed, her head dropped.

Lance reached out and lifted her chin, forcing her eyes to meet his. Neither spoke, neither dared move, afraid to destroy the beauty of the moment. The clock ticked the seconds away and finally chimed the hour, breaking the spell.

Stephanie stirred reluctantly and said, "We'd better eat, Lance."

He nodded his head and answered, his voice husky with emotion, "Perhaps, we'd better."

They took their meal in silence. When they finished, Lance gathered the dishes and placed them on the tray while Stephanie put her coat and mittens on. He carried the tray and walked to the door with her. When they reached the door he turned, the tray between them, and looked deeply into her eyes. His darkened with emotion; hers caught the dancing firelight.

"I won't see you in the morning."

"This is goodbye?"

"I don't like goodbyes," Lance responded.

"All the same it is," she gently insisted.

"I guess so."

"For how long?"

"I don't know. Even a day will seem like an eternity."

Stephanie pressed his lips with her fingertips and shook her head. "It's in God's hands."

"And us?"

"Us, too. If we're meant for each other—if He means for us to be together—then He'll work out our differences."

She reached for the tray, and their hands touched. Fire and ice collided.

"What if He doesn't?"

"Then we'll have to trust that we—you and me together—would have been a miserable mistake—for both of us."

Misery blazed in Lance's eyes, and he groaned, "How can you be so trusting, Stephanie? So passive?"

She looked up at him, her eyes shining brightly through a veil of tears, and said, "Because I know He loves us more than we even love each other."

A particle of hope ignited within Lance, and the misery left his face. His eyes caressed hers. Spellbound, he saw in her eyes the struggle between joy and pain. He recognized the emotions the camera had captured weeks before. But now, seeing, he understood and was humbled.

thirteen

A dozen long-stemmed roses arrived for Stephanie. Tears stung her eyes as she read the card, "May God grant us a lifetime of memories, my darling."

Tears turned to laughter when she noted the signature, scrawled boldly in his own handwriting, "Your Lance." Did he think she still worried about Alana? How could she after last evening?

She glanced in the mirror. Could this be the same Stephanie Haynes that had been afraid of love? Eyes illumined with a soft tenderness peered back at her. She trusted Lance. He loved her. In fact, she hadn't given Alana DeLue another thought—until now.

Stephanie's fine brows knit together, and she turned from the mirror. She gathered the roses to her and, putting her nose down into their crimson, velvet petals, sniffed the delicate fragrance while her mind wandered. Lance hadn't explained what she had seen through the window. She closed her eyes, and the scene appeared as real as it had that night.

If it hadn't been Lance, and she knew that it wasn't, then who? One of the crew? No, Alana remained aloof, having very little social contact with them, or anyone, for that matter. Her only outlet had been her trips to town, but there was no man in Emerald Cove that could interest a beautiful woman like Alana, or could there? Incredulity washed over Stephanie's face as understanding dawned.

Stephanie's face was not the only one to register disbelief that cold November evening. Thousands of miles away in a sun-warmed solarium on the California coast, Lancelot Donovan sat across the table from Alana DeLue. Anger and shock contorted his features as he exclaimed, "You're mad, Alana. I'll. . .I'll—"

"No, Darling. I'm in love."

"With Jay Dalton?" Lance growled, shaking his head in disbelief.

Alana nodded, a half-smile frozen on her face. "Surely you of all people can understand. You feel the same way about that little country girl, Stephanie."

"Don't compare what I feel for Stephanie with what you call love."

"Oh, Lance. Don't be so melodramatic. Love is love, wherever one finds it."

"I didn't come here to discuss the various definitions of love, Alana. I came here to discuss our agreement."

"And we have, darling. I just told you my terms. Take them or leave them."

His eyes narrowed, his breathing ragged, Lance protested, "We had an agreement."

"But I can no longer honor it. My circumstances have changed." Alana smiled, and stretching like a cat, she added, "And so have yours."

"Yes, thanks to you!" Lance's voice rose in frustration as he wrestled with his rising panic. He knew better than to negotiate a business deal in the white heat of anger, but Alana had played her hand well.

"May I ask you why?" His words cut the air, his voice now more controlled, icy.

"Because Jay wants it that way, and he's my husband."

Lance stood abruptly and walked to the window. The blue waters of the Pacific sparkled in the sunlight. From this distance it looked deceptively placid, harmless, but when he turned his eyes toward land, he saw where the destructive power of the surf had eroded the shoreline until, one by one, the houses had fallen into the sea. Some day in the future when the stress became too great and the last vestige of foundation had been worn away, even the house he was standing in would fall, destroyed by that very thing it sought—the beauty and magnificence of the ocean.

Suddenly Lance felt tired. Anger drained from him. His shoulders drooped. Alana called his name, but it fell on deaf ears. He saw in the awesome, tragic splendor before him his own life. If he turned around and agreed to Alana's terms, the beauty of success would be his. But at what price?

Lance clenched his fist and pounded his other hand with it. The price? His own soul. And Stephanie.

He turned back to the dark-haired beauty behind him and said slowly, "Now let me get this straight. You want me to film the rest of the movie here?"

Alana nodded.

"And you want me to cancel my lease with Stephanie? And to place a lien against the property for the amount I have invested in it?" He paused, almost choking on the words.

She nodded. "And Stephanie Haynes is to be replaced in the picture."

"I can't do that, Alana."

"Do what?"

"Submit to any of those demands."

"Very well. Then give up your option and lose your entire investment—which I happen to know amounts to all you have in this world, Lance." She shook her head. "You shouldn't have acted so foolhardily, dear. It isn't like you."

"Nor is this like you, Alana. Why? Why?"

"I told you. Love."

"Love doesn't destroy another person."

"If you mean Stephanie, it won't destroy her. She's young and beautiful, a survivor. But she's standing in the way of something the man I love wants, so she'll have to move over."

"How can you love a reptile like Jay Dalton?"

Fire touched the liquid brown of Alana's eyes. "Careful, Lance, he's my husband."

Lance shrugged his shoulders, "Okay, how did you come to fall in love with your husband?"

"Lance, have you ever lost someone you loved?" The hard glitter left Alana's eyes, and they became softer, more vulnerable.

"Not yet," Lance muttered.

"It's torment—the loneliness, the memories. I thought I'd go out of my mind the months after Brian died. Nothing helped. I couldn't work, I couldn't sleep—pills didn't help. I'd take trips only to remember the times we'd gone there together. I'd see someone who looked like him and the tears, the unending tears, would start again. Finally I couldn't stand it any longer so I walled up my emotions and refused to feel anything. This went on for months. I don't know which was worse, the feeling or the not feeling." She shuddered.

Unwelcome compassion for Alana crept into Lance's heart and for a moment he found himself trying to understand her pain. This was the Alana he knew.

She looked up at him and smiled the dazzling DeLue smile, softness evaporating with it, destroying any vestige of empathy that Lance felt.

"My agent had to talk me into that Las Vegas engagement last summer. It was there that I met Jay, and he made me laugh again. He unlocked all those good emotions that I had thought were over, and it was wonderful. When I went to Boulder Bay, we took up where we left off." She smiled, a faraway look in her eyes, remembering. Then the softness hardened. "He told me we had to be discreet because you and that little self-righteous girl of yours didn't approve of him. The stress of loving him and keeping our relationship secret was too much for me, so I flew home. Jay followed the next week, and we were married."

Lance growled something unintelligible, his eyes burning into hers.

Alana sighed and continued, "Now I'm in a position to help him get what he wants. You're a good friend, Lance, but Jay is the most important thing in the world to me." She paused and looked up at him, her eyes pleading for understanding. "Don't you understand? I'd do anything for him."

Lance groaned, "Alana, you *are* mad. You attempt to destroy another person just to satisfy one man's greed."

"No, Lance. Don't you see? As soon as this picture's a success, you can make it up to Stephanie. It's going to be a smash. What's one little old country inn compared to what you'll have to offer her after this? Besides this wouldn't have happened to her if she'd been reasonable with Jay, but she wasn't. He really needs that property. She doesn't. She has you," Alana rationalized as she leaned toward him, her eyes imploring him to agree.

"She won't want me if I accept your terms."

"Oh, don't be silly. She might pout, but if she really loves you, it won't matter. If she doesn't, then you don't need her anyway."

A cold knot formed in Lance's stomach, and he turned to leave. Even in his turmoil he could see further argument would accomplish nothing. He needed time to sort things out, to bring sanity back. Suddenly the room felt close, the air heavy. His breathing came hard. White-hot anger returned, boiling in Lance until he feared he'd lose control if Jay Dalton walked through Alana's door. Lance left the room without another word, but echoing through the chamber of his mind was another day and another room, and the cold voice of Jay Dalton saying, "I always get what I want."

Lance walked the streets for hours. Later, he didn't even know where he'd been. He'd simply tried to outdistance the torment which drove him.

When darkness fell and the city lights glittered, Lance came to himself and hailed a taxi. It was a mystery to him how he'd arrived back in Los Angeles or what he'd done with his rental car. He hoped he had turned it in somewhere.

He sighed and leaned back in the seat. Tomorrow he'd remember. Tomorrow he'd have an answer to this mess. Tonight he'd rest. Suddenly he felt a longing like physical pain. An image of Stephanie's face swam before his eyes. He couldn't bear it, the wide-eyed innocence of the woman who trusted him. He moaned in the darkness, and the driver heard.

"Hey, buddy, you all right?"

"Uh, yeah," Lance lied. "I just remembered a call I need to make." Suddenly, Lance knew he hadn't lied after all. That's what he needed. To hear her voice, to assure her everything was going to be all right—maybe to assure himself? He could bear anything if he could hear her voice.

Lance rushed through the lobby of the hotel and up to his room. Opening the door, he didn't even take off his coat before he had the telephone receiver in hand. He dialed one digit, then two, before he looked at his watch. It was late, after midnight, but not nearly as late as it was on a lonely New England coast.

In his mind's eye, he could see the inn. The house was dark, and inside, upstairs in her room. . . . He'd never seen her room. His heart pounded at the thought. He felt bereaved, robbed of the comfort of her presence. With a groan, he fell across the bed face down.

Lance slept the sleep of total exhaustion and awoke to morning light streaming in his window. He sat up with a start, forgetting where he was, startled at the strange room, a strange bed. Then he remembered, and he fell back against the pillows with his hands over his eyes. Shut out the world, close down his thoughts. He had rested—the bright light of day blinded him—but his problem remained.

Somehow, somewhere, he'd find an answer. He always had. First he'd call Stephanie. Then he'd settle his problem.

Lance climbed out of bed and reached for the phone. The need to talk to Stephanie was like an unquenchable thirst. The phone rang three times. He drummed his fingers on the table. It rang two more, and he sat down on the bed. Three more times, and he dropped his head in his hand and tapped his foot nervously.

A man's deep voice answered. He recognized Todd's slow, Texas drawl. Irrelevantly he thought how persuasive Todd must be in a courtroom with that pleasant voice. He said curtly, "Todd, let me speak to Stephanie."

"Sure, Lance, right away." No pleasantries, no time wasted—Todd sensed the urgency.

A brief pause seemed like an eternity. Then her voice called out to him. "Lance. Stephanie, here." As if he didn't know, as if he couldn't pick her voice out of an angel choir.

"Darling," he paused. He couldn't go on. How could he inflict her with his pain?

"It's bad news, isn't it?"

"You're not to worry. I'll take care of it, but, yes, Alana is being very unreasonable, and her demands would affect you, and--it isn't only Alana, you see it's—"

"Jay Dalton." Stephanie interrupted him. The two words like an icy, steel dagger fell from her lips.

"Yes, how did you know?"

"Yesterday, I thought about the scene in the cottage. Then I remembered Abby telling me she had seen them together. When she told me, I had dismissed it as mistaken identity until our talk. Go ahead, tell me about it."

"Promise you won't worry?"

"I know whatever decision you make will be the right one, Lance."

The pain in his chest bore down. The burden of her trust was too great. Then he told her the story, leaving nothing out. She'd have to understand his problem, all the implications of his decision, the loss he faced. He expected a reaction—tears or anger, maybe.

His news was greeted with total silence followed by one long, shuddering sigh. "Poor, poor Alana," Stephanie said. "How awful!"

Poor *Alana*? Had the entire world gone mad?

Then Stephanie explained. "She loves him. Lance, he's set her up. He'll destroy her."

Lance muttered under his breath, "She deserves it."

"Darling, she can't help it. That's what I meant. When a woman gives her heart to a man, she's in his power. That's a woman's nature—to submit to the man she loves. That makes her vulnerable. Don't you know that's what I've struggled with all these months? What I've been afraid of?"

Stephanie's words didn't register in Lance's heart. He needed a solution, some sort of action. Who cared what *caused* his problem. The question remained: What could he do about it?

Lance crossed his arms over his aching chest impatiently. "Stephanie, we need to address our problem, not Alana's."

"I know, Darling. What do you think your alternatives are?"

"Pound the pavement in search of other financing."

"What if you can't find any?"

"I will. I *have* to."

"I hope so. You'll keep in touch?"

"Yes. I'll call you soon as I know something. It might be several days. I have a lot of contacts I can make."

"I understand. I'll be waiting."

The line clicked, and he was alone again. Why hadn't he

comforted her? Strangely, she didn't seem to need it. Where were the reassurances that he was going to give her? He didn't have any. Why hadn't he told her he loved her? Because he couldn't. He hadn't earned the right. As long as Alana's offer stood unrenounced, how could he be free to love Stephanie?

Lance pounded the pavement for a week. His efforts were fruitless. The tinsel town which had embraced him as her golden boy now closed her heart and her pocketbook to him.

The word was out. The movie was in trouble, the option running out. No one wanted to take the risk. Rumor ran the gamut—his supporting cast was ineffectual, especially the mysterious beauty he'd discovered. The answer was always the same: Thanks, but no thanks. Sometimes they said it with a friendly reluctance, other times with a cold, harsh no. Either treatment netted the same result.

Lance attempted to borrow the money, but his assets were already tied up in the picture, and the lenders considered the production itself too great a risk to accept as collateral.

Friday night arrived. The next day he had to give Alana an answer. Reluctantly, Lance reached for the phone. He knew the hour would be late, but he had to tell Stephanie—had to explain that there was no other way.

She answered the first ring. Yes, she had been sitting by the phone, and yes, she knew he'd call.

In a flat, emotionless voice, Lance relayed the facts. He only had two options: Alana's ultimatum or financial disaster. If he chose the latter, he'd never be able to work in Hollywood again. His credibility would be gone. Someone had seen to that; they had spread the word.

Lance heard Stephanie take a deep breath. He knew she was fighting tears. Were they for her or for him? She didn't know what his decision was.

He rubbed his forehead with his fingers, undecided as to what to do. What had seemed such a cut-and-dried decision a week ago had changed. But how? The price of his success—had it lessened?

Stephanie began to speak. His heart contracted. He could hear the effort it was taking her. "Lance, what have you decided?"

"What do you mean?" he hedged.

"I want you to listen to me." She took a deep breath ,and her voice strengthened. "The decision you make--I want you to make it as if I didn't exist."

"You can't mean that, Stephanie," he disputed.

"Lance, I love you. The most important thing in the world to me is your happiness. If finishing this film is what you need to make you happy, then that's what I want for you—at any price."

"What about Boulder Bay Inn?"

"We'll borrow money until we get on our feet."

"You can't with a lien against it. That's the whole deal. Dalton knows you can't keep Boulder Bay Inn if I accept their offer."

After a long silence, she spoke softly, emphasizing every word. "Then so be it. You are more important to me than Boulder Bay Inn or anything else in this world. All I want is your happiness."

Lance had a difficult time understanding. She had spoken the words he had most wanted to hear. She not only loved him, but she had freed him to make his own choice.

"Stephanie, Alana did have a point. She said when this movie is a success, we could buy a dozen other places like Boulder Bay Inn."

"Perhaps, but that isn't the point, Lance. The point is you make your decision on what is best for you. I have total confidence that you'll make the right choice. Now I've got to go. And Lance, I love you."

Lance paced the floor all night. He knew that one phone call would seal his future. He reached for the phone. If he called Alana, the success for which he'd worked so hard would be his. He knew that this new agreement would open up broader avenues of promotion. That alone could spell success or failure. Slowly, he replaced the receiver.

He shook his head, and the pacing began again. What other choice did he have? If he turned them down, Stephanie would still lose Boulder Bay Inn. She couldn't survive without the money from the movie production, and without Alana's money, there would be no film. Either way they would lose. Wouldn't it ultimately be better if they accepted Alana's offer and at least salvaged his investment? So what if Dalton won? Wasn't compromise the essence of life?

Lance reached for the phone again, but his fingers stiffened. He buried his head in his hands, and the raging war within tore at him through the night.

Lance was not the only one who faced the pink and gold of a sleepless dawn. While darkness still gripped his world, Stephanie bundled up in warm clothing and went to sit on their bench and face the eastern horizon, fighting a battle of her own.

Memories of that first evening with Lance intruded,

bringing a sad smile to her lips. They had been so full of promise for the future. That dream had become a reality, at least the physical aspects of it had. Now she surveyed her world as the light of the new day bathed it in a soft, shimmering radiance.

The beauty of Boulder Bay Inn dazzled. Thanks to Lance's foresight and her hard work, they had met their goal and surpassed it. Now Jay Dalton might win, after all. Through Alana, all this could be his. Stephanie's heart fought to deny what her mind acknowledged.

She had meant every word she'd said to Lance the night before. The decision involved more than just her. It meant Lance's future, his happiness. She couldn't let her wishes stand in the way of his success, his happiness. But in the blackest hours before dawn, doubts and fears bombarded her.

Stephanie sighed. Maybe she should have pled with Lance to turn Alana down, to trust God to work things out. No, she smiled ruefully, she was the one who had to trust God to work things out. What had she said? If Lance made decisions just to please her. . . .

Stephanie got up slowly, her feet stiff from the cold. She walked toward the lodge. Her friends needed to know about these events. After breakfast, Stephanie called a meeting around the large, old harvest table. She filled everyone in on the decisions to be made and the apparent hopelessness of their situation.

Abigail fumed while Martha and John sat tight-lipped and silent. Todd stroked his chin thoughtfully and finally said, "Let me do some checking, Stephanie. Maybe I can come up with an alternative."

"I appreciate that, Todd, but I can't think of one. If

Lance decides to accept Alana's terms, then of course there are none."

"Did Lance tell you how much he needed to pull this movie off?"

"Several million dollars, especially if he has to hire another star."

"I see, well—"

"Todd, you know Lance isn't going to turn Alana down," Abby interrupted. "Success means too much to him. We had a long talk the night we went to the movie. He loves Stephanie, but his career is everything to him. Stephanie, why didn't you just demand that he turn Alana down? After all, you have some rights."

"I really don't, Abby. All this," and Stephanie waved her hand to indicate their surroundings, "is a result of Lance's money. Without it, the bank would own it, or Jay Dalton. I really don't have any right to make demands on Lance. What it would amount to is my telling him that my career is more important than his. Is that love?"

"Well, is it love for him to sell you down the river?" Abby's eyes danced with an angry fire, then regret clouded them. "I'm sorry, Steph. You're right, of course, and I know Lance loves you."

"Yes, he does, but that's not the question. He must decide what he's going to do with his life. That is more important than this place or. . . ." Stephanie hesitated, her voice faltering, "or our love. I had to release both the inn and Lance to God."

The logs burning in the fireplace sizzled as the fire licked up the sap, breaking the deathly quiet that followed Stephanie's words. Finally, Martha reached in the pocket of her snow-white apron for a handkerchief.

When she had finished wiping her nose, Martha stated, "Stephanie, don't worry about us. The good Lord hasn't let us down yet, and He's not planning to now—I oughta know, I've had a good many years with Him—more than I'd admit to."

Laughter broke the heavy silence as a fragile hope revived in the hearts of the friends. Stephanie stood up. "Okay, troops. Let's get busy. We're not out of a job yet. Todd, I want you to hitch up the sled. We're going to cut a Christmas tree. I feel like trimming one tonight. Martha, you make some special goodies, and we'll just have a celebration."

True to Stephanie's word, they found the perfect tree and, with worries momentarily put aside, gathered in the parlor to decorate it with antique ornaments from the attic. Expectancy filled the air as Todd brought a ladder up from the basement and they began.

Laughter, mingled with carols from the radio, rang through the house. The aroma of spiced cider and gingerbread sharpened appetites. Finally the tree was trimmed except for the star on top. Todd asked Stephanie to do the honors. She slowly climbed the ladder and paused before putting it in place.

With her friends laughing gaily in the background, their glass cups clinking as they drank the warm, refreshing beverage, Stephanie paused to look at the exquisite ornament. Tears dimmed her eyes, and she felt a deep loss that Lance was not able to share this simple joy with her. She groped for the top of the tree and put the star in place, then backed down the ladder, never realizing the cheerful sounds of the room had stopped.

With the bittersweet memory of Lance still blinding her,

Stephanie missed a step and fell. Alarmed, she reached out to clutch the ladder but missed. Suddenly, strong arms caught her, and she buried her face into the warm embrace of a memory turned real.

"Lance?" she whispered in unbelief.

He smiled his familiar lopsided grin and nodded. "Yes, Darling—Your Lance, and God's."

The days before Christmas were the happiest of Stephanie's life as Lance shared his renewed faith whose dimensions were forged in a lonely California hotel suite. In the darkness, he had cried out for direction in a decision he seemed powerless to make. When he had admitted his own inadequacy, the answer had come, gently and clearly. The price of his ambition was too high to pay, and he had walked away from it all, not looking back.

The peace and joy he experienced as a result mystified him. How could he relinquish what had driven him all his life, and not be destroyed?

Stephanie smiled. "That's real faith, Lance. You've been obedient, now it's God's turn. He'll show you, us. I know He will."

With all that was happening, Christmas Eve seemed almost anticlimactic. Lance, Stephanie, and their friends turned the lights off except for the tree and sat around the fire. Todd recited the Christmas story, and they all sang a few carols. Then they opened their gifts. With laughter and teasing, they admired and appreciated what they received. Finally, the floor lay bare beneath the tree, the paper and boxes discarded.

Lance turned to Stephanie with a mischievous light in his eye and said, "The best for last." Pulling her to her feet, he dragged her to the archway between the hall and parlor where a large ball of mistletoe hung tied with bright red ribbon. Todd and Abigail, John and Martha watched wide-eyed and laughing.

Stephanie's face turned scarlet as Lance pushed her in the doorway. Slowly, he enfolded her in his arms, then kissed her lightly on the nose. Her eyes flew open in surprise, to gales of laughter from her friends.

Lance had something in his hand, "Stephanie, do you remember one time I told you I wanted to lay the world at your feet?"

She nodded, the amusement leaving her eyes.

"Well, Darling, I probably will never have a world to lay at your feet, but would you take my heart instead? Will you agree to being an innkeeper's wife?"

Like a flame filling a lantern, love filled Stephanie with a sparkling radiance.

"Oh, yes. That's all I ever wanted, Lance."

Opening the small box, he asked, "Will you wear this ring? It was my mother's."

Against the dark velvet, a large, pear-shaped diamond caught the light from the hallway and sparkled with inner fire.

"Yes. It's beautiful!"

There was a moment of silence, and then Todd spoke. "Congratulations, old man. You've got a real winner there." Holding his cup toward Lance, he continued, "To my good friend and business associate."

Lance's brow furrowed in puzzlement.

Todd smiled. "I was going to wait until Monday, but I can't. I've been in touch with some of my contacts in Texas, and I think we have the backing you need to finish your picture.

Lance's mouth gaped. "You're kidding."

"I wouldn't kid about something this serious, Lance. Can you find another star and get the film finished before your option runs out?"

"Er, yes. I know two or three women who wanted to play that part. One of them would play it a percentage basis rather than for a fixed fee."

"Great, you contact her tomorrow. We're in business."

"But you don't know how much I need."

"You'll have enough," Todd smiled.

"Who? How?"

"I went beyond the sphere of Jay Dalton. These backers are wealthy, Texas businessmen. I simply presented your case. They know the type of films you make, and they said to go ahead. There was only one stipulation. I had to invest as well, to show my good faith."

Lance couldn't speak. He dropped his head, embarrassed at his deep emotions. Finally, he tightened his arm around Stephanie and said, his voice husky, "Thanks, Todd."

Looking toward Abby, Lance confessed, "You were right. God can do a better job with our lives than we can, if we just trust Him with them."

A Letter To Our Readers

Dear Reader:

In order that we might better contribute to your reading enjoyment, we would appreciate your taking a few minutes to respond to the following questions. When completed, please return to the following:

Karen Carroll, Editor
Heartsong Presents
P.O. Box 719
Uhrichsville, Ohio 44683

1. Did you enjoy reading *Free to Love*?
   ☐ Very much. I would like to see more books
      by this author!
   ☐ Moderately
      I would have enjoyed it more if _____

   _____

2. Are you a member of *Heartsong Presents*? Yes   No
   If no, where did you purchase this book? _____

   _____

3. What influenced your decision to purchase
   this book? (Circle those that apply.)

   Cover   Back cover copy

   Title   Friends

   Publicity   Other _____

4. On a scale from 1 (poor) to 10 (superior), please rate the following elements.

___Heroine   ___Plot

___Hero   ___Inspirational theme

___Setting   ___Secondary characters

5. What settings would you like to see covered in *Heartsong Presents* books?

_____

_____

6. What are some inspirational themes you would like to see treated in future books?_____

_____

_____

7. Would you be interested in reading other *Heartsong Presents* titles?   Yes   No

8. Please circle your age range:
Under 18   18-24   25-34
35-45   46-55   Over 55

9. How many hours per week do you read? _____

Name _____

Occupation _____

Address _____

City _____ State _____ Zip _____

······ Heartsong ······

ROMANCE IS CHEAPER
BY THE DOZEN!

Any 12 *Heartsong Presents* titles for only $26.95 *

Buy any assortment of twelve *Heartsong Presents* titles and save 25% off of the already discounted price of $2.95 each!

*plus $1.00 shipping and handling per order and sales tax where applicable.

HEARTSONG PRESENTS TITLES AVAILABLE NOW:

____HP 1 A TORCH FOR TRINITY, *Colleen L. Reece*
____HP 2 WILDFLOWER HARVEST, *Colleen L. Reece*
____HP 3 RESTORE THE JOY, *Sara Mitchell*
____HP 4 REFLECTIONS OF THE HEART, *Sally Laity*
____HP 5 THIS TREMBLING CUP, *Marlene Chase*
____HP 6 THE OTHER SIDE OF SILENCE, *Marlene Chase*
____HP 7 CANDLESHINE, *Colleen L. Reece*
____HP 8 DESERT ROSE, *Colleen L. Reece*
____HP 9 HEARTSTRINGS, *Irene B. Brand*
____HP10 SONG OF LAUGHTER, *Lauraine Snelling*
____HP11 RIVER OF FIRE, *Jacquelyn Cook*
____HP12 COTTONWOOD DREAMS, *Norene Morris*
____HP13 PASSAGE OF THE HEART, *Kjersti Hoff Baez*
____HP14 A MATTER OF CHOICE, *Susannah Hayden*
____HP15 WHISPERS ON THE WIND, *Maryn Langer*
____HP16 SILENCE IN THE SAGE, *Colleen L. Reece*
____HP17 LLAMA LADY, *VeraLee Wiggins*
____HP18 ESCORT HOMEWARD, *Eileen M. Berger*
____HP19 A PLACE TO BELONG, *Janelle Jamison*
____HP20 SHORES OF PROMISE, *Kate Blackwell*
____HP21 GENTLE PERSUASION, *Veda Boyd Jones*
____HP22 INDY GIRL, *Brenda Bancroft*
____HP23 GONE WEST, *Kathleen Karr*
____HP24 WHISPERS IN THE WILDERNESS, *Colleen L. Reece*
____HP25 REBAR, *Mary Carpenter Reid*
____HP26 MOUNTAIN HOUSE, *Mary Louise Colln*
____HP27 BEYOND THE SEARCHING RIVER, *Jacquelyn Cook*
____HP28 DAKOTA DAWN, *Lauraine Snelling*
____HP29 FROM THE HEART, *Sara Mitchell*
____HP30 A LOVE MEANT TO BE, *Brenda Bancroft*
____HP31 DREAM SPINNER, *Sally Laity*
____HP32 THE PROMISED LAND, *Kathleen Karr*
____HP33 SWEET SHELTER, *VeraLee Wiggins*
____HP34 UNDER A TEXAS SKY, *Veda Boyd Jones*
____HP35 WHEN COMES THE DAWN, *Brenda Bancroft*
____HP36 THE SURE PROMISE, *JoAnn A. Grote*
____HP37 DRUMS OF SHELOMOH, *Yvonne Lehman*
____HP38 A PLACE TO CALL HOME, *Eileen M. Berger*

(If ordering from this page, please remember to include it with the order form.)

··

·······Presents·······

___HP39 RAINBOW HARVEST, *Norene Morris*
___HP40 PERFECT LOVE, *Janelle Jamison*
___HP41 FIELDS OF SWEET CONTENT, *Norma Jean Lutz*
___HP42 SEARCH FOR TOMORROW, *Mary Hawkins*
___HP43 VEILED JOY, *Colleen L. Reece*
___HP44 DAKOTA DREAM, *Lauraine Snelling*
___HP45 DESIGN FOR LOVE, *Janet Gortsema*
___HP46 THE GOVERNOR'S DAUGHTER, *Veda Boyd Jones*
___HP47 TENDER JOURNEYS, *Janelle Jamison*
___HP48 SHORES OF DELIVERANCE, *Kate Blackwell*
___HP49 YESTERDAY'S TOMORROWS, *Linda Herring*
___HP50 DANCE IN THE DISTANCE, *Kjersti Hoff Baez*
___HP51 THE UNFOLDING HEART, *JoAnn A. Grote*
___HP52 TAPESTRY OF TAMAR, *Colleen L. Reece*
___HP53 MIDNIGHT MUSIC, *Janelle Burnham*
___HP54 HOME TO HER HEART, *Lena Nelson Dooley*
___HP55 TREASURE OF THE HEART, *JoAnn A. Grote*
___HP56 A LIGHT IN THE WINDOW, *Janelle Jamison*
___HP57 LOVE'S SILKEN MELODY, *Norma Jean Lutz*
___HP58 FREE TO lOVE, *Doris English*
___HP59 EYES OF THE HEART, *Maryn Langer*
___HP60 MORE THAN CONQUERORS, *Kay Cornelius*

Great Inspirational Romance at a Great Price!

Heartsong Presents books are inspirational romances in contemporary and historical settings, designed to give you an enjoyable, spirit-lifting reading experience. You can choose from 60 wonderfully written titles from some of today's best authors likeLauraine Snelling, Brenda Bancroft, Sara Mitchell, and many others.

When ordering quantities less than twelve, above titles are $2.95 each.

LOVE A GREAT LOVE STORY?

Introducing Heartsong Presents —
Your Inspirational Book Club

Heartsong Presents Christian romance reader's service will provide you with four never before published romance titles every month! In fact, your books will be mailed to you at the same time advance copies are sent to book reviewers. You'll preview each of these new and unabridged books before they are released to the general public.

These books are filled with the kind of stories you have been longing for—stories of courtship, chivalry, honor, and virtue. Strong characters and riveting plot lines will make you want to read on and on. Romance is not dead, and each of these romantic tales will remind you that Christian faith is still the vital ingredient in an intimate relationship filled with true love and honest devotion.

Sign up today to receive your first set. Send no money now. We'll bill you only $9.97 post-paid with your shipment. Then every month you'll automatically receive the latest four "hot off the press" titles for the same low post-paid price of $9.97. That's a savings of 50% off the $4.95 cover price. When you consider the exaggerated shipping charges of other book clubs, your savings are even greater!

THERE IS NO RISK—you may cancel at any time without obligation. And if you aren't completely satisfied with any selection, return it for an immediate refund.

TO JOIN, just complete the coupon below, mail it today, and get ready for hours of wholesome entertainment.

Now you can curl up, relax, and enjoy some great reading full of the warmhearted spirit of romance.